SUPER GIRL

Book 4

John Zakour & Katrina Kahler

Copyright © KC Global Enterprises Pty Ltd

Table of Contents

Book 4

The Expanding World

Road Trip

I sat in the high-speed hover plane that belongs to my dad's company, pondering over how much my life has changed this year. When the year started, I was a normal everyday kid living with her mom. I hadn't seen my dad in years. I had learned to deal with that by mostly not thinking about it. Plus, Mom and I had a good life together, and we were a team.

Then I hit the big one-three, thirteen, the teen years. Little did I know at the time that meant I had absorbed enough energy from the sun to become Super Teen. Yep, me…nice normal, Lia Strong, suddenly became a superhero. I'm so strong that a whiff of my feet can knock out a mall. I can lift a building without breaking a sweat. I can jump super high and far. I've been practicing hovering, and I have heat vision and super breath. I can, with practice, even use my scent to make people do what I want them to do. Pretty much, I am a one girl army. Yet the thing that is most different in my life, is that my dad is back.

Turns out, my dad is the head man of BM Science. It's a huge company that invents all sorts of nifty inventions, like this hover plane I'm flying in. Now that I'm super, my dad wants to help me use my powers for good deeds. He and my mom have been great trainers for me. Mom teaches me how to act like a super person, while Dad uses his company to help me use my powers where they are really needed.

That's why right now we hovered over Africa. Until today I had never been more than 100 miles away from my hometown of Star Light City. And I now found myself sitting in the passenger seat of a really sweet plane next to my best buddy Jason.

Jason knows everything about superheroes, so he has become my official consultant.

In front of us sat Dad and his beautiful assistant, Hana. From the way Dad looked at Hana, I could tell he thought of her as more than an assistant. I could almost see the hearts in his eyes. I tried not to think about the fact that Hana was an android Dad had made. Yep, my dad had made his own beautiful assistant who he now had a crush on.

"Doctor Strong, we will be over the drop site in two minutes," one of the pilots informed my father.

Dad swiveled his chair to face me. "You've got this, honey!"

Jason could barely sit still. "Your first mission outside of the country! I'm so excited, Lia!!"

I smiled at him. "I just hope I can handle this."

Jason patted me on the shoulder. "You've so got this, girl! Fifty rhino poachers don't have a chance against Super Teen!"

"I hope so…" I said.

Jason looked me in the eyes. "I know so! I may not be super like you, but I do know super when I see it!" His eyes popped open. "You know, I've been thinking about another defensive ability for you. I'm betting you could hypnotize people."

"I have the pheromone thing going on with my sweat that can make people do what I want, kind of," I said slowly.

Jason grinned. "Yeah, I know, but that's almost impossible for you to control."

"I'm working on it!" I said defensively.

Jason leaned back and held up a hand. "Yes, I understand, but even at best, that's a power that will blast everybody. I think you can do a more controlled one. What about getting a person or animal to focus on your finger moving really fast while using a commanding super voice."

I looked at him. "That sounds pretty comic-book-like…"

"You do have super farts, and you've knocked people and animals out with morning breath…" Jason laughed.

"Good point," I sighed. I lifted up a finger and put it in front of Jason's eyes. I moved my finger rapidly back and forth and said in my most commanding voice, "Follow my finger."

Jason's eyes locked on my finger, following right and left, left and right. I saw Jason's eyelids start to droop. "You will cluck like a chicken!" I ordered.

"Cluck! Cluck!" Jason said, even using his arms for wings.

He squatted down.

"You're Jason again!" I said quickly before he tried to lay an egg.

Jason shook his head. His eyes popped open. "Did it work?"

I smirked.

Dad came over to me. "Okay, honey, we're almost over the drop site."

"Tell me again why we're doing this," I said to Dad.

Hana smiled. "The government of this country wants to stop these poachers, but they don't have the resources. Your father volunteered our services. Once you take out the small army of bad guys, the government will come in and take them away."

"We're over the drop site, sir!" one of the pilots announced.

I stood up. "MAC, activate my suit!" I told my computer assistant that Dad had built for me. I think of MAC as a really smart watch.

"Roger!" MAC said. "I am so excited."

I saw my holographic mask appear in front of my face. My nano clothing morphed into a really pretty light green, sleeveless body suit. The side door to the hover plane popped open. I leaped out and started falling to the ground.

"Since you are immune to sunburn, I thought the sleeveless look would be a nice touch!" MAC said as I fell through the air.

"It is," I agreed.

I took a deep breath. I held out my arms and my legs. My fall slowed to a glide. I smiled. My body rippled with joy! I felt amazing as I slowly descended towards the ground with the wind in my face.

All of a sudden, I spotted my target. It was a campsite of canvas tents surrounding a bunch of men with big guns and bigger trucks, sitting and standing around a table. They looked like they were getting ready to move. To the north, I spotted a majestic herd of rhinos. No way would I allow those men to hurt the rhinos.

I steered myself towards the camp. I kicked my legs. I'm not really sure why, but it seemed to help. My super hearing picked up the voices of the men making plans.

"Okay we will circle the rhinos and then open fire on my count," one of them said.

I had heard enough. I straightened my arms and legs into the diving position. I dove into the ground and landed right in the midst of the group. I hit the hard surface with concussion force that sent the men sprawling. Leaping to a standing position, I quickly dusted myself off.

Pointing at the men, I announced firmly. "I'll give you

guys one chance to surrender!"

They drew their weapons.

"Why should we surrender? We have you outnumbered 50 to one!" a man holding a pair of binoculars smirked.

I took a deep breath to clear my head and calm my nerves. I knew I had this, but that still didn't stop me from being nervous. After all, I had never done anything like this before. I pointed up to the sky. "Look, dudes, I just dropped from the sky." I pointed to the crater caused by my landing. "The ground took way more of a beating than I did." I paused to let that sink in. "Now, unless you guys want me to do to you what I did to the ground, you'll just give up."

The lead man shrugged. "We have weapons."

I shrugged back. "I am not impressed. But in the interest of fair play, I will give you guys first shot."

I stared down the barrels of the biggest guns I had ever seen. I had done the practice simulations in dad's lab. I felt pretty certain these guns couldn't hurt me. Dad says I am pretty close to being completely invulnerable. I'm not quite sure if that meant I could deflect bullets from 50 guns. Pretty sure it did.

The boss poacher, who looked more like a soldier than a hunter, smiled. "You're nervous, I can tell."

I nodded. "Yep, I'm nervous about hurting you all too much."

The boss shrugged. "Look, we don't want to fight you. Leave now and we'll let you go!"

I shook my head. "Not going to happen!" I stomped my foot on the ground.

The force of my stomped ripped through the ground and sent them all reeling backward.

"Tell you, what, I'll make you guys the same offer. Swear you'll never hurt rhinos and run away now. Then I'll let you go!"

A couple of the smarter guys tossed down their guns and ran away. But most of them stumbled back to their feet and stood their ground. The boss glared at me. "Neat trick. Let's see if you're bulletproof!" he said. "Fire!" he shouted.

I heard the sound of about forty high-powered weapons firing at me. I saw the bullets coming towards me. I could trace the path of each one and dodge them if I wanted. While that would certainly be impressive, I figured it would be more sensational to let the bullets bounce off me instead.

I held my breath. I stood there as each bullet hit me then fell harmlessly to the ground. Truthfully, I kind of impressed myself with that.

I rubbed my hands together. "O-kay, you can't say I didn't give you jerks a chance!"

I shot forward at super speed. I decided to save the boss for last. I grabbed the second nearest bad guy's gun. I bent it in half. Then I tapped him on the forehead. He fell over, out cold before he even knew what had hit him. I grabbed the two guys next to him. I smashed them together like cymbals and let them drop to the ground. I raced at the next four or five men at super speed. Each time I took their guns, tied them in knots, then tapped each man on the forehead, knocking each one out. After dealing with the first ten or so, I stopped for a moment, just to take in how the other bad guys were reacting.

They all started to panic and aimed their weapons aimlessly. If I had let them fire, they would have all shot each other. Instead, I inhaled then exhaled, hitting them all with super breath. I hadn't eaten for a while, so I figured my breath probably wasn't very pleasant. The force of my breath knocked them over and the less than pleasant smell knocked them all out.

"Sorry, I forgot my breath mints," I told their unconscious bodies.

Turning my attention to the boss, I smiled as I walked towards him. "I thought I'd save the worst for last."

He instantly dropped to his knees, reaching into his back pocket and pulling out a wad of money that was thicker than a deck of cards. He then waved it at me. "Look, I have a lot of money! It's all yours if you just fly away now!"

I placed one finger under his chin and lifted him off the ground. "That's the problem with people like you, all you care about is money! I don't want your stinking money! I want to do the right thing!" Then I smiled. "And I think I can help you do the right thing!"

The man shrugged and shook his head. "Nah, kid, I'm a pretty bad dude. I don't think there's anything you can do to change that. Just knock me out and turn me over to the authorities, then be done with it."

"I appreciate your honesty!" I told him.

He pulled a knife from his sleeve and plunged it into my neck. The knife snapped. I shook my head. "If bullets don't hurt me, why do you think a knife would work?"

He shrugged. "Like I said, I'm a bad guy. Didn't say I was overly bright. Just brighter than my men…"

I shook my finger in front of his eyes. I noticed how he followed my finger and waved it in front of his eyes very quickly. "Follow my finger," I ordered in my most commanding voice.

The man did as he was asked. His eyes darted back and forth, all the while locked on my finger.

"You are getting sleepy!" I ordered.

"I am getting sleepy…" he repeated slowly.

"Sleep!" I ordered.

His eyes shut and his head dropped forward. I smiled.

"When you wake up you will become a rhino activist. You will do whatever you can to help rhinos," I ordered.

"But I'll be in jail…" the man muttered.

"Well, you can work over the internet while you're in jail!" I replied.

"I obey!" the man said.

I let him drop.

"Man, that felt good!" I said to MAC.

"Yes, nice use of super-hypnosis," MAC said. "You did such a good job that I'm almost afraid to mention this."

"Ah, MAC! Mention what?" I said, looking at my watch interface.

"All those bullets spooked that heard of rhinos. They are now charging a nearby village."

"Oh, that is so not good..." I gulped.

"Agreed! I estimate they will reach the village in three minutes."

"Which way are they going?" I asked frantically.

"East!" he said.

"I'm going to need more help than that." A little arrow pointing left appeared in the watch face and I leaped up into the air.

Dear Diary: Why is it that even when I do something right, I do something wrong? You would think being super would be easier than this!

Rhinos

I jumped into the air towards the charging heard of rhinos. My super-vision locked in on the pack. I saw a dozen large gray rhinos running in fear, their stomping caused a giant dust cloud. I could have spotted them even without super-vision. Further in the distance, I saw the little town that was directly in the path of the stampeding rhinos. The homes were small wooden shacks and there was no way that those homes could stand up to a rhino.

"Okay MAC, any suggestions on how I can stop a herd of charging rhinos?" I asked.

"I'm calculating right now," MAC replied.

"Well," he continued slowly. "You could release a super fart over them. That will stop them cold in their tracks. The trick is calculating wind direction and speed. You will also drop the town you are trying to protect. But knocking them all out is better than having the villagers stomped on."

MAC was right. I had to use one of my super farts. I squinted my eyes and tried to force my butt cheeks to let one rip. Nothing. Nada. Zilch. Of course, it was one of the few times in my life that I actually wanted to fart in public and I wasn't able to.

"Anytime now…" MAC instructed impatiently.

I squinted harder, pushed harder and squeezed my fists. Not sure why I thought that would help.

I shook my head. "I don't have it in me," I sighed for a moment, then crashed to the ground just a few yards in front of the charging pack.

Shooting back up to my feet, I lifted my arm up in the air to halt the rhinos. With nothing better to do, I shouted, "Stop!"

Yeah, I knew rhinos couldn't understand English, but I thought maybe the force of my voice would have an impact.

The lead rhino stopped in its tracks. Could my voice have worked? The rhino abruptly turned blue.

Then, without warning, it rolled over with its legs up in the air. And one by one, each rhino stopped, gasped, and then flipped over.

"That works too," MAC said.

It took me a moment to figure out what happened. I sniffed my raised underarm. Woo, that had a kick to it. I think it even made my eyes spin. Yep, the pressure of fighting fifty armed bad guys and then stopping a charging herd of rhinos had burnt through my deodorant.

"I suggest you put your arm down unless you want these poor rhinos to wilt and never recover," MAC added.

I quickly thrust down my arm and walked towards the lead rhino. His stoMACh was rising and falling, and I breathed a sigh of relief. I was fairly certain he and the others would wake up in a few hours.

"Do you think I need to drag them all away from the

village?" I asked MAC.

"I don't believe so," MAC told me. "When these rhinos regain consciousness, they won't have the energy to do much except wander back to their field. You did it, Lia! You saved the day!"

I smiled weakly. "Yep, I guess so."

"Your dad says…great job! Now report to the hovercraft so that he can get you home in time for dinner. After all, tomorrow is the first day of school!" MAC stated firmly.

"Oh great," I said. "I can hardly wait!"

Dear Diary: Wow, my first road trip mission was a pretty big success. I'm amazed by how much my power is growing. A whiff of my underarm stress sweat can drop a heard of rhinos. Part of me thinks, 'WOW, that's so cool'. Another part thinks, 'YIKES! I could be really dangerous.'

The Plane

With the job done and both the poachers and the rhinos dealt with, I figured it was time to get home. I leaped up towards the plane, keeping my right arm extended to steer me into the open door. I knew I'd have to lock my arm to my side the moment I entered, or else my scent would quickly overpower everybody on the plane.

The plan was simple…get on the plane, then hit the shower ASAP.

I entered through the open doorway and the door whirled shut behind me. I forced my arm to my side. But when I turned, I saw Jason, my dad, and the two pilots instantly go limp.

"Oops, I must smell worse than I thought…" I said.

"Stress sweat can pack quite the punch," MAC replied. "I hold myself partially to blame since I gave you a sleeveless suit. If only I hadn't been such a slave to fashion, then I could have added sleeves and the nano anti-smell bots might have been able to keep up with you…" MAC computed for a second more. "Of course, if I had done that, you might not have stopped the rhinos, so I now conclude that I did the right thing."

The plane shook, then started dropping towards the ground.

"Okay, maybe not," I said.

"Hmmm, one of the unconscious pilots must have their head on the descend switch," Hana said, standing up. She calmly walked towards the cockpit. "It's a good thing I have no need to breathe and I can fly this plane. Otherwise, all the regular humans on board would be in big trouble."

Hana walked into the cockpit and pushed the lead pilot off his seat. She sat down in front of the controls. I felt the plane lift upwards and then hold steady. Hana looked over her shoulder. "Now you go take a nice refreshing shower, Lia. We'll talk girl to simulated girl when you're finished."

The second the cooling water from the shower head hit my head and I felt myself tingle. Ah, I had no idea how much dirt, grime and sweat my body had covering it, but it felt so good to wash it all off. Although, I guess I did know how much sweat there had been, since a whiff of me, even with my arms down, overpowered all the regular people on our aircraft.

"Make sure you wash extra-long under your arms," Hana told me over the intercom. "It's nice that all the men are napping now, but we do want them to wake up before the trip is over."

"I understand," I grumbled back. Though truthfully, I was upset that Hana thought she needed to remind me of that.

"Sorry if I am being over-cautious and telling you the obvious," Hana continued, "it is just what I do."

I added a bit of extra soap under my arms and scrubbed a bit. I then lifted them so the spray could rinse them off. I took it as a good sign that the spray head didn't melt when I pointed my underarm at it. It's a weird feeling of power when your underarms can melt a showerhead. Luckily, that only happened once.

I finished showering, dried off, and then used my super deodorant generously under each arm. I headed to the front of the plane. Hana sat in the pilot seat, using the pilot as a footrest.

She looked at me, saw my expression and shrugged. "Your father made me shorter than I would like, so I'm using the pilot to prop my legs up. Don't worry, I took off my shoes, and my feet aren't stinky at all." Hana motioned to the co-pilot's seat. She had moved the co-pilot to the floor next to the seat, so I stepped over him and sat down.

"I'm glad we have this little time alone," Hana said slowly.

"Ah, me too," I said even slower. "But what's going on?"

She smiled at me.

I pointed at her. "Look you're not going to challenge me to a fight like your previous model did! That didn't work out too well for her as I reduced her to scrap metal."

Hana laughed. "We're not made of metal."

"Well, scrap, or whatever," I said.

Hana leaned towards me. "I just want to have some girl talk…"

Sitting in the co-pilots chair. I looked down at the white fluffy clouds below us. It felt funny to be flying so high especially with an android pilot who wanted to chat. But, pretty much everything about my life felt weird these days. "So, what do you want to talk about?" I asked.

"Your father," Hana said quickly.

"Ah, okay. He's a cool guy. A little on the nerdy mad scientist side, but I know he means well. I mean, if he insulted you or something, I'm sure it was a misunderstanding. Human interaction isn't his strong point."

Hana laughed. "How true, which is why I am glad I'm not human. And it's also why I would like to ask your father out."

"Excuse me?" I said. For some reason, I felt my face blushing.

Hana looked me in the eyes. "I find your father interesting, and funny, and I enjoy being around him. I want to see more of him…"

"By more of him, you mean?"

Hana giggled. "I want to see him out of the office. I want to go bowling with him. Watch Netflix with him. Go out to dinner with him!"

"Do you even eat?" I asked. Yes, I know that shouldn't have been my main concern just then, but I wanted to know.

"I have no need to eat, but I can eat for fun. My e-stoMACh acids can dissolve food into energy much like humans do. Except I have no need to poop or pee."

"Too much information, Hana. Too much information!"

"Right! Sorry. It's my job to give information. I forget that with you humans, it's possible to give too much information for your little brains," Hana replied.

"Okay, let's get back on topic, please. Does my dad know about this?"

Hana grinned. "No, when it comes to matters of the heart or e-heart, your dad is pretty clueless."

"So, Dad didn't make you want to be his date?"

Hana laughed. Her laugh somehow sounded like birds chirping. "Of course not, your dad made me only to be a tool. A tool that can grow. That's what I am doing."

"Okay, if Dad made you only as a tool then why did he make you so...."

"Hot?" she asked.

"I was going to say built like a supermodel."

Hana grinned. "Oh, please. The average supermodel weighs 110 pounds, and I weigh 120 pounds."

"So, the answer is no then?" I said.

Hana shook her head. "Nope, your father has no idea I am thinking this way. He will be surprised, but hopefully pleasantly surprised. I'm sure at first he may go out with me simply as an experiment to see how I will react."

I nodded. "Yeah, he can be a big nerd. The first time he came back into my life, he attacked me with a drone."

"Yes, I heard." Hana's eyes opened wide. "But it is my hope that he will grow to see me as more than an invention. I hope he will learn to love me."

"Wait...love?" I stammered. "Are you able to love?"

Hana's eyes widened even more. "I hope we will all find out soon enough. Even though I know you can't hurry love."

"So, you're asking for my permission to date my dad?" I asked.

"I thought it would only be proper," Hana nodded.

"And if I say no?" I shot her a curious look.

Hana's eyes became smaller. "I will be sad. But I will still ask him out once I win you over. I just compute it will be easier on all of us if you agree."

"Then go for it!" I said. "I hope you and my dad will be happy together. But I'm definitely not calling you, Mom!"

"How about mother-2.0?" Hana asked.

"Nope. Definitely not!!!"

Dear Diary: Just when I think life can't get any stranger, my dad's android assistant asks me for my permission to date him. Yeah, sure it's strange, but I just want my dad to be happy. Just because he and my mom didn't work out, doesn't mean he doesn't deserve happiness. I hope it works out for him.

Back in the USA

By the time the hover plane landed, Jason, my dad, and the pilots had all regained consciousness. And I actually made it home before Mom did, which was kind of weird. Mom is never out past 9 PM, so I texted her:

LIA>Mom u ok?

MOM>B home soon honey.

'Well, that was cryptic', I thought to myself.

My ever-faithful dog, Shep, walked over and I gave him a nice scratch behind the ears. I think he enjoyed that so much, he might have even purred. Since I still felt pretty fresh from my hover plane shower, I kicked my shoes off. I wanted to spend my last night before school as comfy as possible.

"Hopefully, a whiff of my shoes won't knock you out!" I told Shep.

He didn't fall over instantly which was a good sign. Still, for some reason, Shep always needed to take a good sniff of my shoes. Apparently, he wasn't as smart as I had always thought. Shep walked towards the spot where my shoes had landed.

"I wouldn't do that if I were you," I warned. "My feet may have been cleaned from the shower, but those shoes had been through a lot today." Shep stuck his big nose right into the shoe then pulled his nose out.

"Phew, I guess they've aired out enough," I said.

His knees began to wobble, and he rolled over onto the ground.

"Oops, I guess they haven't aired enough after all," I shook my head at Shep. "I did warn you!"

I heard the front door open. Mom walked in wearing a red dress, a very short red dress.

Mom pointed at Shep. "That dog will never learn!" she smiled.

I stood up. "Wow, Mom!" was all I could say.

She opened her arms and spun around.

"Did you have an event at the hospital?" I asked.

She leaped over and sat on the couch, then kicked off her red high-heeled shoes and wrinkled her nose. "Phew! If Shep wasn't knocked out by your shoes, mine would certainly put him down. I could sedate patients with those. Heck, I could sedate the entire hospital." She looked up at me and grinned, "Guess I was nervous."

I finally put two and two together, and my face lit up. I shot over next to her. "Wait, you were on a date?"

She looked at me and smiled. "Yes. I hope you don't mind."

"Of course, I don't mind! You deserve to be happy!" I said, taking her arm. "Who's the lucky guy?"

Mom didn't answer. She turned away smirking.

"Come on Mom, spill."

"I met him at the hospital…" she replied slowly.

"You're dating a patient?"

She shook her head and laughed. It felt good to hear my mom laugh. "No, he was putting together a news story on what makes medicine work!" she said.

"So, he's a reporter? I didn't think they had newspaper reporters in this town. Is he from out of town?"

"He is a reporter and he is from this town, but he works for the TV station. It's Oscar Oranga!" mom said.

"You mean the Oscar Oranga who is always reporting on Super Teen? The man who has made it his mission to discover who Super Teen is?"

Mom nodded. "Yes, I'm afraid so. He's very dedicated and also very nice."

"But Mom! He's like my arch nemesis!" I said, admittedly being overly dramatic.

Mom smiled. "Don't be silly. He's just doing his job. You don't have an arch nemesis. You're a teenage girl, not a comic book character. Besides, if you did have a nemesis, it would be Wendi Long!"

"Good point," I added.

I thought carefully about what to say next. After all, I did want Mom to be happy. I just couldn't be sure we could trust Oscar Oranga. "Do you think he might suspect that I could be Super Teen? Do you think he might be dating you to get information? Reporters can be tricky when going after a story."

Mom looked at me with raised eyebrows. "What your mom can't get a man on her own? I'm a doctor, and I'm still pretty fine looking if I do say so myself."

I put my hand on her arm. "Mom, you know I think you're beautiful. But this seems awfully suspicious. I mean the man is always asking, 'Who is Super Teen?' Now he's dating Super Teen's mom."

She smiled at me. I knew that smile meant - *Honey, I'm not nearly as dense as you think I am*. Then she spoke the words, but they weren't exactly what I was expecting to hear. "Honey, I thought the same thing. So, when he asked me out I put him under."

"You did what?"

"I used my hypnotic voice on him," Mom said.

"Hey, that's cool, I just used mine today!" I said, getting slightly off topic.

"Yes, it's a handy power, but one I don't like to use too much, or else I might make everybody around me just roll over and be quiet for a while."

I nodded. "I know the feeling."

Mom put a finger under my chin and lifted my head up gently. "These powers of ours are a blessing. We can do a lot of good in the world, either openly or behind the scenes.

Still, we have to be careful not to become dependent on them or abuse them. That would be very bad…"

I put my hand on her shoulder. "I know, Mom. I'm careful."

She grinned. "I don't like using the hypnotic command voice, but when it comes to my daughter's safety I will. So, I questioned Oscar, and he really only wants to go out with me because he finds me smart and also very attractive. Her grin grew. "His words not mine." She put a hand on my shoulder. "You are always first in my book."

I leaned in and kissed her on the cheek. "Love you, Mom."

"Love you too my girl."

"So how was the date?"

She leaned back in the chair and smiled. "Let's just say there will be a second date!"

"Good for you Mom!" I truly was happy for her. Now both my parents would be dating. What a coincidence!

"How was your trip?" Mom asked, changing the subject.

"You know me, same old, same old. I took out a small army of rhino hunters, accidentally knocked out a heard of rhinos, and then knocked out everyone on the hover plane with my nervous sweat. All in all, mostly successful."

She laughed. "Yes, nervous sweat can have quite the kick. I think it's part of our superhuman defense mechanism. It's painless for people we put to sleep and lets us get on with our job."

Mom and I spent the rest of the evening chatting. I didn't mention that Dad's android assistant wanted to date him. I figured it was best to see where that went before mentioning it. After all, Mom and Dad were friends now, so there was no use tossing more information out just in case nothing came of it. But even so, it was a huge coincidence that the dating thing was happening in both their lives at exactly the same time.

Dear Diary: Wow, my mom and dad are both possibly dating other people. Well good for them. Maybe with a new year starting at school, something will click for me as well. Who knows? Maybe Brandon will finally see that Wendi isn't good enough for him. Or maybe I will meet somebody new! But then, there's always Jason. Yeah, he's my BFF but sometimes I still wonder if maybe, just maybe, there might be more between us. He knows me so well. But there is no need to rush. I'm not old like Mom and Dad. I have plenty of time to sort this all out, and I'm sure the right boy for me is out there.

I just wonder who it will be.

Schooling

The next morning Jason and I walked to school, just like we had done each day since we were six. I liked our walk time together. It felt warm and reassuring, like a nice snuggly blanket. Plus, it gave us a chance to talk about life.

"So, I thought the mission went well yesterday," Jason told me.

"Me too, but sorry for knocking you out."

Jason chuckled. "Ah, I'm used to it now."

"It's just amazing how much our lives have changed in the last year," he continued. "Wow, I'm best buddies with Super Teen. Your dad is back in your life. We know other super people. It's all so cool."

"Yeah, it's pretty amazing!" I agreed as we passed by Ms. Jewel's house.

Sure enough, her mean dog, 'Cuddles' started barking and running towards the fence that surrounded the house. Cuddles happened to be the worst named dog in the world. Nothing sweet about this dog! He rushed towards us until he either saw or sniffed it was me then he stopped dead in his tracks and rolled over with his legs up in the air.

"It's nice Cuddles has learned he's no match for you," Jason grinned.

I smiled back, "Yep, it does save time."

We walked by Felipe's and Tomas's house. Normally Felipe would come out to greet us. But not today.

"That's weird. No Felipe," I said to Jason.

Jason shrugged. "Maybe he's sleeping in. After all, he is getting older."

I looked at their house. "Funny, I don't sense them in there."

Jason pulled me along. "They could be on vacation or out shopping. Even half-vampires need to eat and shop and relax."

"Good point," I nodded, as we continued on our way.

Even though I hadn't been too keen to go back to school, now that we were on our way, I was eager to get there. It was always fun arriving for the first day. The school was still as ugly as ever, but it was clean and smelled fresh. Janitor Jan always did a great job preparing the place. I always wondered how one woman could clean such a big school until I learned she was a sorceress. That made perfect sense in this new world of mine.

As soon as we arrived, my good friend, Krista rushed over to me. She had her hair curled and it looked great. "Big news! Brandon isn't running for class president because he wants to concentrate on his grades and his LAX," she said in one breath.

"How is that great news?" I asked.

"Because Wendi is running!" Krista said hurriedly.

I shook my head. "Krista, I'm still not hearing the good news part…"

"I have to agree," Jason said.

Krista took a deep breath. "Well, I didn't want Wendi to run unopposed because, well, she's Wendi. She's on enough of a power trip already!"

"So, you're running against her?" I asked.

Krista laughed. "No, I could never beat Wendi. I nominated you! Steve Mann seconded it. And then Marie thirded it."

"Ah…" I said. I felt honored but also a bit overwhelmed. I had a lot on my plate. Plus, I knew the candidates for class president would have to give a speech in front of the entire class. I hate giving speeches. My knees were shaking just thinking about it.

"Of course, Mr. Ohm, our class advisor says none of this matters until you agree. So, do you agree?" Krista asked me, her eyes batting away.

Before I could respond Wendi sauntered over. "So, Strong, I heard a rumor that you think you can beat me for class president," she sniggered. "I'm a better LAX player than you. I'm smarter than you. I'm prettier than you. I'm more popular than you."

"Yeah, well…" I stuttered.

"Oh, good comeback!" Wendi replied. "Yep, you have what it takes to run the class," she snorted.

I fought the massive urge to blast Wendi with heat vision. Or, maybe use super voice to make her think she's a chicken or my pet poodle. But no, that's not how good guys do it. We do it the right way. We let the people pick their leaders.

"Well, Wendi," I said, slowly locking my eyes with her perfect blue ones. "Guess we'll let our classmates decide because I'm definitely running against you!"

Krista jumped up and down applauding until Wendi stopped her with a glare.

Wendi held out a hand. "Well then, may the best girl win!"

I shook her hand.

Yeah, I can stop a small army of bad guys. I can drop a charging pack of rhinos. However, something told me this would be my toughest test yet. I knew I could do it. At least I hoped I could do it.

Wendi walked away with her posse. Jason and I headed to my locker so I could store my jacket. Standing next to my locker was a short stocky kid with braces and glasses. His name was Steve Mann.

"Ah, ah, hi Lia," he said slowly like he had trouble thinking of the words.

31

"Oh hi, Steve."

He looked at me and then began tapping his foot. Glancing shyly away, he murmured, "Ah, you know I seconded your nomination for class president."

"Thanks, Steve."

Jason came straight in, "I would have done it if I had been here." "Only my BFF and I were still walking into school together like we always do!"

Interesting. I got the impression Jason was hinting to Steve to stay away. Although Steve didn't seem to pick up on that.

"You know Lia, the school has a dance this year," he stared directly towards me.

"Yep. They have one every year. Though it's more of a listen to music, talk and stand around…"

"I'd love it if you'd go with me!" Steve blurted suddenly.

"Steve, the dance isn't for like six months!" I replied.

Steve nodded. "Yeah, I know." He looked down.

"Has somebody else already asked you?"

"No of course not, because the dance is still six months away," I repeated.

His eyes popped open. "Great! So, you don't have a date?" He looked at me eagerly, like a puppy expecting a treat.

I really didn't want to go to the dance with Steve Mann. I didn't mind that he was a bit of a nerd. It's just that he happened to be shorter than me. Plus, to be honest, I had never really even said three words to Steve before this. I had no idea why he was so keen for me to go with him.

"Look, Steve, let me think about it for a few months," I said slowly.

"That's not a no!" Steve said, his voice cracking.

"No, it's not a no…," I said even slower.

Jason leaned past me. "But it's not a yes either!" he told Steve.

Steve smiled and turned and walked away humming. "I have a chance! I have a chance!"

I sniffed my underarm. Had I forgotten my deodorant? Had my pheromones been firing extra hard? Nope, I smelled like spring flowers. Certainly not my natural scent.

Jason locked his eyes on Steve's back. "That kid bugs me. Always talking about how his computer is so fast, how he has a cool drone, how he's going to go to MIT and will invent the next Google." He looked at me, "You're not *seriously* thinking about going to the dance with him, are you?"

I'd never seen this side of Jason before. I do believe he was jealous. "No, I just didn't want to hurt his feelings," I replied.

Jason breathed a little sigh of relief. Then the bell rang, and we headed to class.

"Of course, if he is going to invent the next Google, I'd be crazy not to at least consider him!" I added, walking into Mr. Ohm's homeroom, a wide grin attached to my face.

The amazing thing is that the rest of my day went pretty smoothly. Sure, I had to listen to a bunch of teachers telling me how their subject was the most important subject in the world. Sure, they would each pile on homework like they were the only teachers in the school. Of course, the hot food in the cafeteria was cold, and the cold food somehow hot. But I went through the whole process with my friends and teammates, and that made everything more fun. Besides, while I would never admit this out loud, I liked learning. Oh, and I'm pretty sure I caught Brandon smiling at me.

After classes, I hit the school weight room with a few girls from the team. Obviously being Super Teen, I didn't need to train in that particular weight room. In fact, I could easily carry all the weights in that room with one hand. My dad's company had a set up a special gym and a weight room for me to train in, along with the other super girls, Tanya, Lori, Marie, and Jess. The company weight room has special ultra-mega weights that weighed tons and I could lift them easily. I only came here to keep up appearances and to bond with my teammates.

Since the weights here also meant nothing to Lori (with her bionics), she and I ran around the room while the other girls used the weights. Marie worked on the bench press while Cindy Love and Michelle Row spotted her up front. Luke Lewis was also there. Usually, the boys don't lift when the girls do, but Luke was recovering from an injury. I think he has a crush on Marie.

Marie was going for a record bench press for her, 100 pounds. Impressive, considering that I don't think Marie weighed 100 pounds soaking wet. Lori and I stopped our running and moved next to the bench to cheer Marie on.

Marie pulled the weight from the rack. She took a deep breath.

"You can do it, Marie!" I said.

"You got this girl!" Lori told her.

Marie guided the bar slowly down to her chest. She took a deep breath. She pushed up. The weight moved up. She let out a breath. She straightened her arms. She locked the weight back in the rack. She sat up. "I did it!" she shouted.

Marie shook her head and beads of sweat bounced off her short dark hair. One of the droplets hit Cindy and she turned to gold. Another drop of sweat hit Michelle and she too froze into gold. A couple of drops hit Luke, who became gold as well. Lori and I spotted beads of sweat coming towards us but managed to dodge them. The sweat hit the ground, turning the floor beneath us into gold.

"Oops," Marie said. "This is bad."

Lori looked at the golden kids and the golden floor. "Marie you could be so rich if you wanted to be!"

"Oh my, this is not good...." Marie said. "I really didn't want to do this."

Tanya Cane walked into the room. "Oh, now I see why Janitor Jan sent me down here. She thought my time control power might be helpful. I see she was right."

Packed

Tanya looked over the situation. "Wow, Marie! That is a cool power!" She tapped Michelle and Cindy. "They are truly solid gold."

I glanced at Tanya. "Can you reverse time to before the accident happened?"

"Maybe," Tanya replied. "But time is very particular. It likes to happen the way it's supposed to happen. So, my guess is if I did it right, Marie would just turn them into gold again. And, if I did it wrong and went back too far, I might turn them all into babies. Which might not be much better. In fact, it could be really messy. Plus, if I do it really wrong, EVERYBODY could turn into babies!" She shook her head. "My power can be tricky to control. That's why I usually just slow down time… It's simpler. I've already slowed down the school, so nobody comes in here and sees this."

"Oh my gosh, this would be so hard to explain," Lori said.

I walked over to Marie and put my hands on her shoulders. I let out a little sigh of relief when I didn't turn to gold. "Marie you did this, and you can undo this," I told her.

MAC spoke up from the interface I wore on my wrist. "I've spoken to your father. He says he'll send a relief team if needed. They can move the golden kids to the lab and work on them there."

"Tell Dad 'thanks', but not necessary just yet. I know Marie can turn them back."

MAC paused for a moment and then informed us, "Your father says he will keep the team on standby."

I locked my attention on Marie. "You've undone this before, Marie. You can undo it again."

"But that was just one person, now it's three of them."

I nodded in agreement. "That is true, but it's still the same concept. I know you've been working on this with Dad's people. You can create a field with your power. You should be able to turn all three of them back at once."

Lori pointed to the floor. "Why don't you practice on the floor?" she smiled encouragingly.

"Lia and I will move the statues close to each other to make it easier for you."

Tanya walked Marie over to the golden spots on the floor. "You can do this Marie!" I called over as I picked up the now solid Luke and moved him next to the two girl statues.

MAC spoke up, "Your father reminds you that you all have a power training session tomorrow. He says that things like this are the reason why we have these weekend sessions."

"We'll be there," I said.

"All of you?" MAC said.

Tanya and Lori both nodded. Marie groaned and said, "Of course I'll be there! I don't want stuff like this to keep happening."

"I noticed from the school records, Jessica is absent today," MAC said. "Do you know if she will be coming?"

I shrugged. "Jess takes her power seriously, so if she's around I'm sure she'll be there. But, let's stick to the problem at hand. We need Marie to turn these kids back!"

I thought about the situation. The last time Marie's power misfired she had been thinking about money for college. Maybe it was the same now. "Marie," I said slowly walking towards her, "Have you been worrying about money again?"

Marie looked at me. Her eyes popped open. "Yeah, I have," she admitted. "I was thinking that I need to get stronger and better so I can get a LAX scholarship to college!"

37

I touched her gently on the shoulder. "That's the key to your power misfiring. When you worry about money you tend to turn things into gold."

"That certainly would help with the money problem," Lori said with a grin.

"This isn't funny, Lori," Marie scolded. "I'm dangerous like this! I'm worried that if I sneeze or fart you'll all turn to gold! Plus, what about having a boyfriend someday? What if I get nervous and turn him into gold?"

"You might have the perfect boyfriend then," Tanya snickered. "He'd be worth a lot of money and he wouldn't talk a lot. Plus, he'd always smell good!"

Marie turned to her. "Tanya don't even kid like that!" she said, poking Tanya on the hand. Tanya's hand instantly turned to gold. The gold then began to streak up her arm.

Marie threw her hand over her mouth. "Oh no!"

Tanya stayed calm. She waved her non-golden hand over the golden one. The skin instantly stopped transforming into gold.

"Whoa!" Tanya said slowly. "This is a weird feeling. I've slowed time around my arm but not sure how long I can hold this."

Marie put her hands on top of her head. "Yikes! I didn't mean to do that. You see, I am dangerous!"

I looked Marie in the eyes. "Marie, you are one of the kindest people I know. You're not dangerous. You just need to learn to control your emotions, which will allow you to control your power."

She stared back at me and her body relaxed.

"Take a deep breath and let it out," I said.

"I'm afraid my breath will turn you into gold!" Marie frowned.

I shook my head. "No, it won't, because you can control this. You can control your power."

She took a deep breath and let it out. I felt her breath

hit my face and then an instant relief when I didn't turn to gold.

"See? I am still flesh and blood!" I told her. "You can control this! Just don't worry about money. Marie, you're a strong player and smart. I'm sure you will get a college scholarship!" I patted her on the shoulder.

Marie smiled. She bent down and touched the gold spots on the floor. They turned back into whatever gray substance weight room floors are made of. Her smile grew. She stood up and tapped Tanya on the hand. Tanya's hand slowly transformed back from solid gold to flesh.

Tanya flexed her hand. "Much better. I know they say being golden is good, but nope, it is not."

I smiled at Marie. "See, easy peasy."

I led Tanya and Marie to the three golden statues. Marie looked at the glistening bodies. "I can do this!" she said. She leaned forward to touch Luke, and then stopped, her hand in mid-air. "Wait, if I turn one person back, how do we explain to them why the others are golden statues?"

"Good point," I told her. "I guess this means you'll have to turn them all back at once."

"You did turn them all into gold at once," Lori added.

Marie leaned back a little. "I can do this. Everything is going to be fine," she said softly to herself. The only reason I heard her was because of my super hearing.

She took a deep breath and exhaled on Cindy, Michelle, and Luke, her breath covering all three. Instantly each of them transformed, and we watched the gold coating fade into normal skin.

"How'd we get over here?" Luke asked, a puzzled expression on his face.

"Yeah, we were spotting Marie over there," Michelle said, pointing to the bench.

Marie laughed a bit nervously. "I made the lift, and then we all came over to this side of the room to try some different equipment. Don't you remember?"

I moved forward, focusing on the three of them. "Yes, that was what happened!" I said, in my most forceful command super voice.

The three nodded. "Yes, that was what happened!" they repeated.

Lori then led the three out of the weight room. "Okay girls let's get going. We'll see you all on Monday."

We all breathed a little sigh of relief.

MAC chimed in. "See, your father is correct! This is why your weekend training sessions are so important."

We all nodded in agreement.

Dear Diary: Wow! That situation could have become really ugly, but luckily my friends and I kept it under control. I'm amazed by the power we each have. I now truly understand the saying, **with great power, comes great responsibility.** *I also figured out that the way to control our powers is through practice and understanding of our powers. We can all be dangerous if we don't learn to control the powers we have. But I have faith in myself and my friends.*

I guess I should be thankful that Wendi didn't come down to check on us. Of course, maybe if she was there, Marie would have turned her into gold as well.

Now, that would have been fun! Wendi would make such a great lawn ornament or scarecrow!

Okay, Lia, wipe those thoughts from your mind.

Practice makes Better

By the time Jason and I got to BM Science the next morning, Lori, Marie, and Tanya were already there. Hana met us at the gate and drove us into the test building. Yep, BMS had made an entire building just for us.

Dad and Hana had Marie working with their team of mind experts. They'd arranged for her to do meditation and yoga to keep her powers under control. We saw Marie in a small white room standing on her head and going "Oooohm". She seemed content.

Next, we walked past a room filled with weights. Lori had two heavy ton weights over her head, as a trainer looked on giving her encouragement. A couple of people dressed in white lab coats were observing Lori's progress. One had a stethoscope around her neck to check Lori's heart rate, and she seemed very surprised at what Lori was capable of.

The other person was holding an iPad to keep track of Lori's results.

"So, what will I be doing?" I asked Hana.

Hana grinned. "We want you and Tanya to have a friendly sparring match. The goal is for each of you to simply stop the other one any way you can."

"Me versus Tanya," I smiled. "I think I can power through her time control and take her down," I said confidently.

Jason looked at me with a frown.

"What?" I asked him.

"Lia don't get overly confident. You have awesome raw power. All the abilities you have makes you super-duper-uber powerful," he said slowly. I could see he was choosing his words carefully.

"Your point?"

He hesitated. "Tanya is older. She's had her power longer and her power...wow... she can control time. That's pretty cool too! If she concentrates her power on you, she can certainly slow you down!"

Hana grinned. "That's an excellent point, Jason, that's why we have you as a consultant."

We entered a room shaped like an octagon. The walls were all covered with mirrors. The floor was padded.

Tanya stood in the room dressed in a pretty blue top, white shorts and electric blue canvas sneakers. She smiled at me. "I see it's you versus me in a friendly little fight."

"I guess so," I said. I had to admit I was a bit put off by her calmness. After all, I am Super Teen. Nothing she could really do could hurt me. Yet she stood there so steady.

Hana motioned us both to the middle of the room. "Now, Doctor Strong, Jason and I will be watching from the observation room. The room will flash red and then you two can begin. Remember this is only practice. The winner will be the one who knocks out the other."

"Wait, I thought we only had to stop each other?" I asked.

Hana looked at me. "I changed the rules to make it more challenging. After all, in a real fight, the rules change all the time." She took Jason by the hand. "Come."

Tanya and I glanced at each other.

"This should be interesting," Tanya said. "I've been working on new ways to use my power."

"Good," I said with a nod. "I'm always trying to improve myself too."

"Have you seen Jess?" Tanya asked.

"Nope, I'm getting a little worried about her."

Tanya shrugged. "She's a witch, she'll be fine."

A red light flashed. I figured I'd take out Tanya fast and easy: dart forward at super speed, a quick nerve pinch, and game over. But I felt myself slowing down. It was like the gravity around me had become so strong, each step felt like my legs weighed a few tons. I gave Tanya credit, she had slowed time fast. Still, that wouldn't be enough to stop me. I kept creeping towards her, even though each step felt heavier than the last.

Tanya moved closer. "I know you're tough and not much can hurt you, but even you have to breathe." She popped a shoe off one foot. "I really feel sorry for you about this. While I can't totally stop you in time, I can slow you down enough." She placed her shoe over my nose. Wow! If my head could have jerked back it would have. "My shoes get nasty if I don't wear socks. I know a quick whiff of this wouldn't normally hurt you. But I am speeding up time around your nose, making it seem as though you've been breathing in nothing but my shoes for a year!"

Tanya removed her shoe away from my nose. She snapped her finger. "Okay, time around you is back to normal."

The room spun around me. My eyes felt so heavy, it was like elephants were trying to force them to close. But I

44

refused to fall. Tanya walked up to me. She tapped me on the head with her little finger. I hit the floor.

"Sweet dreams," were the last words I heard.

I came to in a bed in a white room, with a doctor looking over me. Dad and Jason were also there. "You okay, honey?" Dad asked.

"Yeah, only my ego took a beating."

"All superheroes have some weakness. Yours is that you have to breathe."

"Hopefully, now you've learned you're vulnerable to gas attacks. The good news is, I am sure if you're prepared for a gas attack, you can hold your breath for a great deal of time!" Dad commented.

Tanya patted me on the shoulder, "Once again, sorry I had to do that. But your dad and Hana thought of it. I'm glad to see you're alright now."

Jason gave me a thumbs up. "Yeah, the MMA Fighter, Samurai and Ninjas that Tanya practiced on last week are all still recovering! Two of them haven't stopped sucking their thumbs. The third drops to the ground and rolls over when she sees Tanya."

"I do leave quite the impression," Tanya grinned.

All of a sudden, red lights began flashing. Sirens started blaring. A voice over the intercom said, "Alert! This is not a drill!"

Dad looked up at the ceiling, "MAC, show us the security feed!"

A TV monitor dropped from the ceiling to the middle of the room for us to see. There in the monitor, we saw Jessica storming into the building. A couple of guards rushed towards her. Jessica pointed at them. The guards instantly began to cluck like chickens.

"What have you done with Felipe and Tomas?" she shouted at one of the security guards. She waved her fist into the camera. "You'd better give them back or else!"

"Oh, this could be trouble…" Dad said.

Dear Diary: Ouch, I finally lost a fight. Sure, I've had my close matches before. But this marks the first time I actually got knocked out cold. I guess it's good that I do have a weakness. It keeps me humble.

Tanya packs a lot of wallop. Her ability to slow time is powerful and her feet pack almost the same punch as mine. I wonder if having natural superpowers give you naturally super stinky feet? Whatever…I now know for sure that I can be taken down, especially if I don't plan before a fight. My brain is as useful as any of my powers!

I just hope we can sort out the issue with Jessica!

Angry Witch = Big Trouble

I sat up in bed. "Dad, what's Jessica talking about?"

Dad took a few steps back. He scratched his head. "I have no idea..."

Standing up, I looked at Hana, "Is there something going on here that Dad doesn't know about?"

Hana grinned. "My dear Lia, there are many things going on here that your dad doesn't know about. We have become a huge organization. One single human cannot track them all. But luckily, I am not human, and I am close to your dad at all times. I also can track them all. We have done nothing with Tomas and that adorable little Felipe."

"We did invite them to train," Dad said slowly. "But they turned us down. So that was that."

"Apparently not," Jason said.

Hana's nose started to twitch. Her mouth locked into a wide grin and her eyes sprung open, with her pupils dilating until the whites of her eyes disappeared.

"Ah, what's going on with Hana?" I asked dad.

He glanced at her. "She's doing a deep search. It's so cute!"

I let that comment slide. I had bigger fish to fry than to worry about my dad thinking his *cute* android.

Hana's nose stopped twitching. Her eyes blinked again, and the wide grin disappeared from her face. "Doctor Donna Dangerfield recently started her own company, Bio Augmented Diversified, and they are doing work like ours. They refer to themselves as "BAD". Their motto is, "Making You a Better You!"

"Where are they located?" I asked.

Hana's nose twitched. It stopped. "No idea. It's very hush, hush."

Looking up at the monitor, I could see that Jess had moved deep into the building and anybody she came in contact with instantly dropped to the ground and began clucking. "Okay, we stop Jess first. We need to explain to her what's going on. Then we find out more about this BAD!"

I looked at Tanya. "You ready for this?"

"You're asking me to take on one of our best friends who is an angry powerful witch? Of course, I am!"

We raced out the door then stopped at the weight room to grab Lori, who had been watching the situation unfold. "This is going to be tough!" Lori said. "Jess has a lot of magical power, but if I can sneak behind her I think I can take her out."

"Let's try to talk her down first," I said. "Nobody wins if we go up against Jess."

We stopped at the lab to get Marie. Both the scientists working with her had been turned to big yellow cheese statues. Marie came over, "Sorry, guys I was hungry and got a little nervous watching Jess."

"Marie you stay here and turn these guys back. We'll use you as our backup plan against Jess if needed."

Marie nodded. "Sounds like a good idea."

MAC used the building guidance system to lead us through the halls towards Jess. The walls of the building were all electronic, so he could display arrows showing us the way to go. He also gave us a constant feed to let us see Jess's actions exactly. The good news is that so far she hadn't vanished anybody. Plus, she hadn't completely turned anybody into a chicken yet. That made me hope we could reason with her.

We met up with Jess who was approaching a big lab filled with scientists who were busy at work, completely unaware of what was going on around them.

As soon as Jess spotted us, she turned towards the scientists who immediately dropped to the floor and began to cluck like chickens. A few of the robot security drones tried to stop Jess but she instantly reduced them to piles of melted metal.

She then glared at each of us. Her gaze made us all shiver.

I took a deep breath. "Jess we need to talk," I said slowly but firmly.

"Tomas, cute little Felipe, and his mom are all missing!" Jess replied.

"Yeah we've heard," I said. "My dad and Hana insist they don't have them."

Jess raised an eyebrow, "You trust your dad? The man who wanted nothing to do with you until you had superpowers and a robot to keep an eye out for you?"

Jess hit a nerve there. She had a solid point, but now wasn't the time to think about my relationship with my dad.

"Hana's an android," I said, realizing that Jason was rubbing off on me. "But yes, you make a good point."

Jess stood there tapping her foot impatiently. "So now what?" She raised her arms over her head.

"If you're trying to knock us out with super BO, it's not working," Lori said.

I held my breath just to be on the safe side, but I felt pretty sure that wasn't what Jess was up to. She wasn't a super BO kind of girl. Sadly, that was one of my moves.

"No, I'm putting a magical invisible shield around me so you can't attack me!"

"We'll see about that!" Lori yelled, leaping across the room at Jess.

Jess stood there, arms crossed. Lori flew towards her then bounced off harmlessly. She rolled into a bunch of scientist chickens, knocking them over like bowling pins.

Lori sat up, "Nope, she's not bluffing."

Tanya whispered to me, "I may be able to freeze her in time, even in that shield. But if I can't, we might both end up as chickens. Actually, once I saw her turn two guys who whistled at her into turnips…"

"I have a better idea," I told Tanya.

I looked Jess in the eyes. "Let's all go talk to my dad and Hana. I'm sure we'll get the truth out of Dad, at least. If they aren't involved, which I'm pretty sure they aren't, they can help us find out who has Felipe and Tomas."

Jess dropped her arms. "Deal."

She sniffed herself. "Good timing, my deodorant was about to wear off!"

Dear Diary: I hate to admit this, but Jess really had a point about Dad. I want to trust him. I need to trust him. But man, oh man, I haven't seen Dad for about ten years, then all of a sudden I'm super, and he shows up at my door. As well as that, it turns out he runs a giant scientific research company that is interested in super beings. Plus, the man built himself a girlfriend, which, I'm sorry, is totally weird. Hopefully, though, he was telling the truth. But I need to find out for sure!

Planning for Action

We all gathered in one of BM Science's lush conference rooms. The room had a long-polished oak table surrounded by the most comfortable leather chairs ever. I assured Dad and his people that Jess wouldn't turn any of them into something weird, as long as they told the truth.

Dad sat at the head of the table with Hana positioned next to him. A fierce-looking security guard stood behind him at the ready.

Though I knew that if Jess lost her temper, there would be nothing that any security personnel would be able to do to stop her, regardless of how fierce or tough he was.

Just as that thought entered my head, three more security people walked into the room. These ones all wore red body armor and helmets. By the mechanical sounds they made when they moved, I knew the armor must have been enhanced.

"Jess, I assure you that my company has nothing to do with the disappearance of Felipe and Tomas," Dad told her.

Jess pointed at the guards. "Then why all the security people in the room."

Hana answered for Dad, "My dear girl, you have reduced half of our staff to mindless chickens. I have called for extra security to be cautious. Mr. Strong's brain is our company's biggest asset. It is my job to protect it."

Jess glared. She snapped her fingers. The red-shirted guards turned into tomatoes. The bionically enhanced guards turned into toy soldiers. "Just to be clear, no amount of guards will help you if I find out that you are behind the disappearance of Tomas and Felipe."

I believe I saw Dad gulp. Hana, though, stood her ground. "Impressive use of power."

Jess nodded. "When I am angry, my power flows freely. That's why I usually try to control it. People don't like me when I'm angry."

Hana grinned. "Good point, but you see my dear, I'm not people." Hana pointed at Jess. A bolt of electricity ripped into Jess. Jess jerked back and forth in her chair. She collapsed.

A team in white medical suits rushed in. They gave Jess a shot in the arm.

I leaped up. "Dad, Hana, what are you doing?"

Hana answered again, "Just protecting my man, honey. Jess is fine. We'll simply keep her sedated until the rest of you figure out who's behind this."

"So, it's not you guys?" Lori asked.

Dad stood up and answered, "No, it is not us. We

would never do anything like this." He looked at Hana.

"I do not approve of you doing that to Jessica! She was scared and reacted. She was defending her loved ones."

"As was I," Hana replied.

Dad pointed at Jess. "Wake her up!" he ordered the medical team. "I have truth on my side. I don't need protection."

One of the docs gave dad an, '*Are you sure about this*?' look.

"Do it now!" Dad ordered.

I'd never seen this forceful side of him before. I think I liked it. Looking at the smile on Hana's face I knew she liked it too.

The medic leaned in and gave Jess another shot.

Jess slowly started to move. Her eyes shot open. "What the?" she said.

I placed an arm over Jess, preventing her from standing. "Jess, calm down, it's a misunderstanding."

Jess shook her head. "My brain feels scrambled. I can't concentrate enough to use my powers…"

"That will wear off soon," Hana told her.

Dad shot Hana a look.

Hana lowered her head. "I'm sorry if I overreacted."

"Let's all get to talking now," I said slowly but forcefully. "We're stronger when we all work together. What do you know about this BAD company?"

"They are very new. Doctor Donna Dangerfield started them just a couple of months ago. According to their web page, their goal is to make the world a better place for everybody," Hana explained.

"Okay, if they have a web page, they must have an address," Marie commented logically.

Jason answered. "They do, but the address is only a PO Box in Moon City."

"So, they are somewhere in Moon City?" Jess asked.

"Possibly," Dad said. "I'll have one of our 'fly on the

54

wall' drones head straight there and keep an eye on their PO Box."

"Fly drones?" Tanya asked.

Dad beamed. "Drones that look like flies. They are amazing!"

"They are!" Jason added.

"So that's all we have?" Lori shook her head in disgust.

"For now," Dad said. "But I promise you, we will get to the bottom of this."

I turned to Jess. I put my hand on her shoulder and looked her in the eyes. "I trust him and so should you."

Jess didn't blink. "I'll give him a couple of days."

Well, that actually went better than I thought.

Dear Diary: Okay, life never gets easier. But I guess learning how to cope is part of growing up. I had to trust my dad would get this done, especially since he had Jason helping. My relationship with Dad might have been shaky for a while (most of my life) but Jason had never let me down. Plus, I knew dad was trying to make things right. I just hoped we could find a solution before Jess went ballistic!

Date

I got home to find a note on the dining room table: "Out on a date. Buy a pizza, on me." Well, at least Shep greeted me with a lick. I bent down and patted him. "Looks like it's just you and me tonight, big guy."

He woofed.

"Actually, I don't mind at all, Shep. We'll enjoy the pizza together!"

My phone started to explode with beeps. I picked it up.

LORI: Turn on TV.

MARIE: Yikes!

TANYA: Turn on TV.

JASON: Yikes!

I turned on the television. I saw Oscar Oranga hiding behind a table. "This is Oscar Oranga reporting from Casa De Amor restaurant where I had my date rudely interrupted."

The camera scanned the restaurant. Everybody there lay on the ground stiff and pale. They were all breathing, but slowly. I saw Mom laying there, quite still. I hoped she was faking so as not to expose herself.

A girl dressed in black, with a black mask, boots, and cape, grabbed the mic from Oscar. She shook her fist at the screen, "Super Teen…I, Glare Girl, challenge you!"

I leaped out the door. I knew where Case De Amor was. Not because I had ever been there, after all, my love life was less than zero, but I had always dreamed of eating there. I was glad mom got to. Even if she did have to face a super bad girl. I leaped into the air. I finally might have an arch-rival, one besides Wendi. I guess I should be happy in a way.

"Should I call the rest of the team?" MAC asked.

"No," I said. "I need them as a backup just in case I lose," I replied.

"Tanya says she's glad she's not out in the open as a superhero!" MAC told me.

"Yeah, it's not a life for everybody," I grunted with a shake of my head.

Arriving at the restaurant, I found Glare Girl sitting with her boots up on a table. Her hands were behind her head and her hair was as dark as her black costume. "Well, well, you're braver than I thought," she commented, still not bothering to stand up.

The restaurant looked amazing: silk tablecloths, flowers, and candles on every table. A band was set up in the corner. But of course, they were on the ground now. All the unconscious waiters were dressed as Matadors. The place smelled of sweet onions.

I forced myself to concentrate on Glare Girl. "What's your deal, girl?" I said.

Glare Girl snickered. "You're just so sweet and wholesome all the time, and I thought the world needed balance. I'm the balance. Not so sweet, not so wholesome. I'm just a hot girl out for fun!" She looked around the restaurant. "Nice place you folks have here in Starlight City! Of course, the people are all a little stiff," she giggled.

I pointed at the people stiff on the floor. "This is how you have fun, terrorizing people?"

Glare Girl nodded. "It is. Besides, at least when I take out a room of people, I do it on purpose, not with super foot odor or a fart. No class or style there."

I stopped walking towards her. "Those were accidents."

Glare Girl snickered. "That makes it worse." She stood up. "Now are we going to give each other manicures, or are we going to fight?"

I flew at her. She focused her glare on me. The

58

pressure of that glare made me feel like I had a hundred-ton weight sMACking me in the face. The air around me heated up, making me feel like I was in a sauna set on NUKE. It slowed me down but didn't stop me. I grabbed Glare Girl and lifted her in the air.

"Is that all you got?" I asked.

A flick of my wrist and I tossed her across the room. She tumbled to the floor. I watched her pause briefly before staggering to her feet.

"How impolite, you never let me answer you!" she said, wiping a bit of blood from her lips. She smiled. I did not like the look of that smile.

Glare Girl stood up. She cracked her neck then reached into a pocket she had under her arm. She pulled out a tiny, little, red-headed girl. And when I say tiny, I mean she had to be one inch tall.

"About time," the tiny girl said. "Whoa, you might want to consider switching deodorants!"

Glare Girl let the small girl float to the floor. "Please, I don't use deodorants. When you're a bad girl you enjoy your own natural scent!"

"Gross!" the tiny girl said.

The tiny girl abruptly grew to normal kid size and I eyed her pink and yellow jumpsuit. Her mask was shaped like an S, for a cool look. She waved to me. "Hi, Super Teen, I'm Ellie Mae...I mean Shrink Girl."

"You seem like a nice kid. Why are you working with the princess of black?" I asked.

Shrink Girl shrugged. "We're cousins. Like they say, you can't pick your family. So, if you let us teleport away now, everybody will be happy. We both have a cool video we can show on YouTube. All the people get to recover. My cousin has had her fun."

I walked towards them slowly. "I can't let her keep hurting people."

Glare Girl laughed. "Nobody is really hurt. I didn't

wilt anybody. I just wanted to test you. I'm helping you be a better you."

"I hate tests! Especially on Sundays!" I said, darting towards them.

I saw Shrink Girl point at me and then take her index finger and thumb and squeeze them together. Suddenly I found myself looking up at Glare Girl who now towered over me.

"Sorry, I had to do that!" Shrink Girl said. "It will wear off soon."

I leaped up into the air and clobbered Glare Girl with a flying uppercut to the jaw. My blow jolted her head back, knocking her to the ground.

"Even small, I still pack quite a punch!" I told Shrink Girl as I hovered in her face.

"Yikes!" she shouted. She turned and quickly made a circular motion with her hand.

"She's tougher than the doc said," Glare Girl whispered to her little cousin. "Get us home!"

"I'm still getting used to this porting power," she whispered back. "I can only go a few miles."

"That will get us home!"

A glowing sphere of silver energy appeared next to Glare Girl. Shrink Girl shrank down again. She darted over to Glare Girl and grabbed her. They both disappeared into the ball of energy.

"We mean you no harm!" Shrink Girl's voice echoed from the energy ball. "Oh, and I can teleport too!" she added, her voice echoing like it was in a tunnel. The ball of energy sizzled, then faded away.

"Yeah, I kind of figured out the teleporting part," I said, feeling my body return to normal size. For a second I considered chasing them, but I realized I had no idea where they had gone.

Mom stood up and came to my side. "Come on Super Teen, help me get all these people back on their feet."

Dear Diary: Well, I guess I've finally made it as a superhero now that I have an arch-rival or nemesis. As powerful and mean as Glare Girl is, I still somehow find her more likable than Wendi Long. Ha, I guess you don't need superpowers to be super annoying. Certainly, this Glare Girl wanted to be a pain in my behind, but I really didn't get the feeling that she hated me. She just wanted to see what I could do and what I could take. I think I gave her a pretty good idea of that. Sure, her glare stung, but it wasn't anything I couldn't handle. Sure, her little cousin Shrink Girl succeeded in miniaturizing me, but that didn't slow me down much at all. Honestly, the girl's teleporting powers seem more impressive to me. Man, that certainly means she would be hard to find. Dad and **Hana** *told me they guessed these two came from BAD. I trusted them, maybe I shouldn't have, but I did. Plus, Glare Girl did mention a doctor. Could that be Doctor Dangerfield? Could BAD be making their own super people? Now, that would be bad. It couldn't have been a coincidence that these two popped up around the same time I was learning about BAD. I had faith I would get to the bottom of this and also rescue Felipe and Tomas. I needed to do it fast though before Jess lost her cool. Plus, I had an election at school to win. Well, if not win, then at least not embarrass myself. The thought of giving a speech made my stoMACh gurgle. Man, if I farted in the middle of a speech that would be bad on so many levels. Wow, being super can make life super complicated!*

My Other Arch Enemy

On Monday, I walked to school in my usual way, alongside Jason. That seemed to be the constant in my life. The one thing I really needed.

"That fight you had yesterday was weird," Jason told me.

I nodded. "Yeah, I know. Being blasted by some sort of glare vision then shrunk down to a tiny size wasn't my idea of a relaxing Sunday evening."

"Have you seen what people think about the battle?"

"Nah, I'm taking some time off Facebook. It's just a place for people to go and say stuff they wouldn't say face to face with anybody. It's just not worth worrying about or wasting my time on…"

"Well, Wendi thinks it was staged to make you look better."

"Of course," I sighed.

"But most people are really thankful you showed up to save the day," Jason added.

"That's nice. I do like to help. But what's your point, buddy?"

"I think this was a test of their powers and your powers. To see how they stack up to you."

"So, do you think these two were made super?" I asked.

Jason nodded. "I do. One was older than you. The other was younger. Yet they were cousins. So, they probably have some trait that makes them easier to turn super. I'm pretty sure BAD is making super people."

"They were from our town," I said.

MAC chimed in. "I've given the recording of your

fight to your father's people for analysis. They noticed that both the girls had slight scars on their necks. Which means…"

"They had implants," Jason answered.

"Exactly," MAC said.

"I just thought of something!" I broke in quickly, unable to mask the excitement in my voice. "The Shrink Girl slipped for a second and called herself Ellie Mae. I figure she has to be nine or ten. If we search nearby areas for a girl with that name, we can talk to her and get a clue. She seemed nice. My super hearing picked up the fact that she can only teleport a limited distance."

"I'll alert your dad's people," MAC said. "I'm sure they will come up with something."

"Great!" I said.

"Until your dad's company finds some information for us, I suggest you concentrate on more normal but just as challenging problems," Jason said. "Have you thought about your campaign yet?" he asked.

I shot him a look. I fought back the urge to hit him with a bit of heat vision. "When would I have had time?" I asked.

Jason grinned. "Good point." He turned and pulled some rolled up papers out of his backpack. "That's why I've done some work for you!"

He unrolled one of the papers and showed it to me:
VOTE FOR LIA!
SHE'S JUST LIKE YOU!

There was an American flag and also our school flag (which I didn't even know we had), under the text. It looked pretty cool.

"It's nice. You know I'm not like anybody else in the school though. Even Tanya, Jess, Marie and Lori aren't bulletproof and super strong. I'm like really super. Heck, I could fart and be the only one left standing in the school!"

Jason laughed. He put an arm around me. "Lia, those

are your powers, those aren't you. You are the person who worries about knocking out the entire school."

"Yeah, that would be bad…" I said.

Jason continued. "You are the person who tries to use those powers to help the world become a better place."

"Yeah, I do."

"You are a person who is constantly trying to figure out what the right thing to do is."

"Yep, that's me."

"You worry about little things like your breath not smelling fresh," Jason added.

"When your morning breath drops your dog, you learn to worry about these things," I told him.

"You have all these cool superpowers that others don't have."

I nodded as we neared the school. "Yep, that's kind of my point. You're making my point for me."

Jason stopped walking and turned me to face him. "But you also still have to worry about…homework, who your parents are dating, what other kids think of you and most importantly what your place in this world is going to be." He paused to let that sink in. "Your super-powers are great, and they let you do fantastic feats, but they come with problems too. They make you different from the rest of us. And that's any kid's greatest fear…being so different they can't find a way to fit in. Which makes you worry about fitting in with the rest of us. That makes you just like the rest of us!" Jason explained. "In fact, you're an inspiration, you're learning how to take your differences and make them work for not only you but also the world. You're fitting in by helping others." Jason stopped talking, out of breath.

"Wow, Jason I've never heard you talk so much."

"It's because you're an important person to me. Watching you inspires me to be a better me. I know you can do that for others as Super Teen but more importantly as Lia."

We walked into the school grounds which seemed very quiet for that time of morning. Usually, there were heaps of kids milling around the front entrance. I wondered where everyone was.

But then I considered what Jason had just said. I felt better about myself than I had for a long time. I felt like I was glowing. I turned to Jason. "I'm not glowing am I?"

He smiled. "Nope, but you're floating a bit."

"Oops," I said forcing myself back down to the ground.

We headed into the building. Out of nowhere, Wendi appeared. I watched her strut over towards us. So much for me feeling good about myself. "I see my worthy opponent has finally entered the school," she said, almost choking on the word worthy.

Looking around I noticed the walls already lined with posters that featured Wendi's perfect face with the caption.

Vote for Perfection!

Vote Wendi!

Dear Diary: Jason helped me to feel so good about myself today. And then I saw Wendi's posters. How am I going to compete with those?

W for the Win

Jason went to work putting up my signs next to hers. Of course, my signs were much smaller and not as flashy. Wendi looked at them with disdain. I'm surprised she didn't put a finger in her throat and pretend to throw up. Instead, she laughed. She turned to her new BFF, Maggie Carr, a tall, athletic looking girl with red hair. "Can you believe that I have to compete against this?" Wendi whispered to her, still loud enough for everybody to hear.

Maggie nodded. "Sure, I can. Those are the rules," Maggie replied confidently.

Wendi gave Maggie a look that said, "Duh".

Maggie fumbled with her words for a second or two, trying to figure out the best way to keep her BFF happy. "But your posters are SO much better. And they're bigger too!" she added.

She then thought for a second. You could tell when Maggie was thinking because she would tap her foot and roll her eyes like she wanted to force herself to think faster. "I think I read on Facebook that the biggest signs always win!"

Patti Queen, a small girl with short brown hair, darted over to Wendi. Patti had a roll of tape in her hand. She saluted. "I've posted all your posters," she told Wendi. Then she half looked at me. "Oh hi," she said as if I should be honored that she'd noticed me.

The three girls turned and walked away. No other words were said. Although Maggie did give a small goodbye wave and a curt smile.

I shrugged and headed to my locker. Of course, Steve Mann stood there leaning against it. "Hi, Lia! What a nice surprise to see you here!" he said.

I pointed to my locker. "Ah, this is my locker."

"I knew that," he said stepping away from it and standing in front of Jason's locker. "Nice day isn't it?"

"Yeah, it is," I said.

"Man, that Wendi is something else, isn't she!" he commented, leaning casually against Jason's locker. He began to slip then steadied himself. "I mean, sure she's good looking if you like that sort of thing. But I like you..."

I stared back at him and frowned.

Before he had a chance to say anything else, Jess came over. "You! Get lost!" she ordered.

Steve's eyes glazed over. He turned and started walking towards the school doors.

Jess groaned. "Ugh, he's being too obedient. He probably will get lost somewhere," she sighed.

"Jess, stop him," I said.

She looked at me. "Well, it would stop him from annoying you!"

"Jess!"

"Yo nerd, I meant go to homeroom!" she ordered.

Steve stopped walking towards the door. He turned and headed towards his homeroom. Jason and a few other kids had their eyes glazed over as well. They too stopped talking and turned and walked like zombies to their classrooms.

Jess grinned. "When I talk, people listen, whether I want them to or not."

"What's going on Jess?" I whispered.

"Any progress in finding Tomas, Felipe, and Felipe's mom?" she asked me.

"You sure his mom's missing too?" I asked.

Jess nodded. "Yes, I've been checking their house daily. They're all missing. But all their stuff is still there. They were certainly taken."

"We have a lead on BAD. My dad's people are

finding the address of one of their test subjects. Then I'll go talk to her," I explained.

"Good! When they get her address, I'll go with you," she replied anxiously. "When will they have it?"

"Not sure," I said. "But I'd better go alone, to begin with."

"Why, Lia? Don't you trust me?"

"Actually Jess, when you're in this mood, I don't. The girl's just a kid. She seems like a sweet kid. Plus, she can't talk if she's a turnip."

Jess dipped her head. She took a deep breath. "You may have a point." She looked at me and thrust a finger in my face. "But as soon as you have BAD's address, you text me! I want to rip that place apart with you."

"I promise," I said. "After all, we're all part of a team. Right?"

She turned to walk away.

"Right, Jess?"

She stopped. "Yes, we're a team," she sighed.

I placed my hand gently on her shoulder. "Good to hear you say that. We're stronger as a team."

She looked down and away from me.

"You know it's true, Jess," I said forcefully, trying to will the words into her mind.

She looked up at me. "I know it's true. But it's hard for me to accept that I need help. Bad for my cool, loner image."

I patted her on the shoulder. "Don't worry, you're still cool!"

Her eyes lit up. "For sure." She turned and headed towards the door.

"Ah Jess, we have school."

She shook her head. "I can't think of school on days like this. It's hard to concentrate. I might slip up and turn my classmates into toads."

I reached out and grabbed her by the arm. "Nope, as

68

being part of that team, I can't let you wander off; school is important. Not just for the learning stuff, but for the social interaction."

She tilted her head. "You don't look like a nerd but you sure talk like one."

"Thanks!" I told her.

The bell rang.

I pointed up. "They're playing our song."

"Nerd," Jess laughed walking towards her homeroom.

I let out a little sigh of relief and raced into my own classroom.

The rest of my school day went pretty average for me. First off, in English, I realized that I'd forgotten to write a paragraph explaining my plans for the year. Luckily, I was able to use my super speed to write it in class. I told Mrs. Dexter that writing it by hand made it more personal. She accepted that. I didn't feel bad about using super speed. I hadn't written the paper on Sunday night because I'd been battling a super kid teleporting girl, and a nasty Glare Girl, who broke up my mom's date with a reporter who was trying to learn my secret identity.

In history and political science, Mr. P asked me what my platform for class president would be. I told him that it was to be a good person and to treat people fairly. A few of the kids laughed, but a few more nodded their heads. I noticed Brandon was one of them. In fact, Brandon even talked to me after class.

He told me he had to vote for Wendi since she was his girlfriend, but he truly wished me the best of luck. That was both sweet and frustrating at the same time.

In gym class, Coach Blue spent much of the class explaining the importance of hygiene to us. Then she made us do push-ups and sit-ups for the rest of the class. Joy. I could handle that. What got to me was that after class, I heard a couple of girls (Lori and Patti) snickering about the hair stubble under my arms. They compared my armpit to a jungle. It looked like I needed to shave.

Dear Diary: I think I'd rather deal with deadly drones, robots, and androids than with some of the mean girls in my class. My body may be invulnerable, but my feelings certainly aren't.

The Pits

At the end of the school day, I fought the urge to leap home in one bound. I have no idea why I let Wendi and Patti get to me so much. But they did. All I could think about were the mean things they said, especially about my underarms. Man, it would have been so good to give them a blast of super underarm odor. That would have made them nice and quiet. Of course, it probably would have also made a lot of other people nice and quiet too. People who didn't deserve to get blasted, just because of two mean girls.

Jason noticed that I was moving at a quicker pace than normal. "Ah, why are we walking so fast, is there something wrong?" he asked, a worried look appearing on his face.

"Or do we have a lead on who that girl is?" he added hopefully.

"No," MAC answered for me. "Lia is upset that Wendi and Patti made fun of the hair growing under her arms."

"Oh right," Jason said, his eyes popping open. "That explains why you're keeping your arms so close to your sides."

I turned to him without slowing down. In fact, I picked up the pace. "It made me feel bad, okay?"

Jason began to jog so he could keep up with me. "Of course. You may be super, but your feelings are regular human feelings." His face turned slightly red and he slowed his pace. "Ah, have you shaved since you've become super?" he asked, chewing his lip with embarrassment.

I shook my head and sped up more. "Nope. But now's the time. I know it's weird, but that's all I can think about now...like how gross my armpits must look. It's ridiculous how I hadn't even thought about this until I heard them laughing. Now it's all I can think about."

"Okay, well, don't you think you should wait for your mom...for like tips and stuff..."

I shook my head. "Nope, can't wait. I've seen her do it. How hard can it be?"

"Ah, well...your mom isn't as invulnerable as you are..."

We stopped in front of my home. "Thanks for your support, buddy. You're a good friend. I'll be back to normal once I get rid of this hair!" I raced into the house at super speed.

Leaving Jason on the pavement to continue alone to his house, I shot inside and gave Shep a quick pat. Then I zoomed upstairs into my mom's bathroom. Tossing open the cabinet, I scanned for razors. Funnily enough, I only saw one pink one sitting in the corner on the top shelf. I grabbed hold of it and could see that it looked unused. I knew my mom

72

wouldn't mind me using it.

I raced into my bathroom. I turned on the water and ran the razor under it. I lifted my arm. I put the razor on my armpit. I thought about the process. I mean this wasn't rocket science. You move the razor down the underarm, lift it up and repeat the process. I lifted my arm. I got a whiff of myself. Ouch. I'd have to shower after this. I ran the razor down my underarm. I looked at my underarm. The hair was still untouched. I repeated the process pressing harder. I looked at it once more. It was still covered with hair. I looked at the razor. Maybe there wasn't a blade. The razor now looked crinkled and bent. It shook and wobbled like it was made of putty. Yep, the razor met my underarm and lost big-time. My underarms had wilted a razor. This was such a feeling of power but also absolute horror. Would I be forced to have hairy underarms and legs forever? OMG, people would call me Wookie!

Wait, wait, no. Mom's legs and armpits are smooth. She'll know what to do. I pulled out my phone.

LIA>MOM OMG I JUST TRIED 2 SHAVE MY UNDERARMS!

MOM>HONEY ABOUT TO GO IN 2 SURGERY TALK AFTER. LUV

That was it. I took a deep breath. Okay, fine, surgery could only last a few hours. I could wait this out for a few hours. Hopefully, there would be no crimes I had to stop, or leads on who the teleporting shrinking girl was. My phone beeped.

JASON>Ah, how's it going?

LIA>Why do u ask?

There was a pause.

JASON>This is kind of awkward but I'm guessing you can't shave...

LIA>OMG how do you know?

JASON>Lia, you're super. Bullets can't hurt you, no way a razor can.

73

LIA>(POOP) OMG! (POOP)

JASON>Use UR heat vision.

LIA>Huh?

JASON>Think about it. Please don't make me say more about this. It's pretty embarrassing.

LIA>OK

I put the phone down. I dropped the razor (well what was left of it) into the trash. I lifted my arm. I locked my vision on the hair. I concentrated and sent out my heat vision. A beam of energy sparked from my eyes. The beam hit the hair, the hair burnt off. It took about three seconds until my underarm was nice and smooth. But way warm. I thought about ice cubes. I blew a little puff of super cool breath on my armpits. Ah, now that felt better. I lifted my other arm. I repeated the process. Yep, I was right. This certainly wasn't rocket science. I lifted up my underarms and checked them out in the mirror. Smooth as glass!

I figured that while I was at it, I may as well do my legs. My legs were actually a little easier since I had a nice clear view of them. I smiled. Now a quick shower and I would be ready for whatever the world threw at me next.

Dear Diary: When you are super it's amazing how the littlest, simplest, almost silly task can become quite the chore. Who would have thought being invulnerable would make it impossible for me to shave like a normal girl? My BFF Jason, that's who! Not only did he realize I had that problem, but he knew an ingenious way to solve the problem. All that comic reading he does sure comes in handy. My lesson from all of this…no matter how powerful you are, you still need friends.

Cat's Out

The next couple of days were pretty normal. Wendi and her gang made their usual taunts and mocked my chances of winning the election. Wendi constantly pointed out that she was better than me in everything, which to her meant, LAX and being pretty. Okay, she also had slightly better grades. That was only because I got a B- in gym class last year. And that was only because I'd been getting used to my powers. So, I took it slow in gym class to make sure I didn't accidentally hurt anyone.

Jason discussed my campaign strategy with me. My strategy was simple. While Wendi talked about being perfect, I talked about being just a normal kid who can relate to other kids. Ha, me normal, now that was something. Although, as Jason had said, I really am normal. I'm just normal with superpowers.

Sadly, there was still no progress finding Tomas and Felipe. I knew we had to do something fast before Jess turned the entire town into turnips. Dad's company still hadn't been able to find Shrink Girl, Ellie Mae. I started to think that maybe we had the wrong name.

But then while walking home on Thursday, MAC came to life. "Finally, finally!" MAC exclaimed.

"They've found Ellie Mae?" I asked, almost panting.

"They did. Her full name is Ellie Mae OPAL. She lives at 1111 Side Street, in Moon City," MAC told me. "The name and address were encrypted, but we broke through."

"Excellent! I'm good as there now!" I said.

Jason grabbed my arm. "Wait, don't you find it a little weird that after days of searching, she suddenly pops up at such a strange address?"

I stopped. "Maybe..." I admitted.

"Don't you think this could be a trap?" Jason added.

"Maybe," I groaned.

"Shouldn't we tell the rest of the team?" Jason asked.

I answered without really thinking, "No, not yet. The others don't even have costumes. It would be weird if these girls from Starlight City just showed up in Moon City. Besides I'm scared of what Jess might do."

Jason nodded. "Good point. Then take me with you instead."

I shook my head. "No way! If it's a trap, I don't want you getting caught or being in danger."

"I can take care of myself," Jason replied. "I've been training with Hana. She says I have natural moves."

My first thought was...is there no man in my life who doesn't have Hana in their life now? I fought back that thought because it wasn't useful. Plus, being jealous of an android was just plain silly.

I looked Jason in the eyes. "If this is a trap. I'll need you and the rest of the team to save me and take out BAD." I told him.

Jason gave me a weak grin. "Got it..."

I activated my costume and leaped into the air. "Ah, Lia, not to chill your cool vibe," MAC said. "But you leaped the wrong direction. Moon City is the other way." A flashing arrow pointing behind me appeared on the screen.

"Oh okay, right," I said.

I landed and turned around. I leaped up in the right direction. I figured four or five super leaps and I should be there. I needed to make a quick decision. Did I want to approach this girl as Lia Strong or Super Teen? I figured Super Teen might be a bit too much. I didn't need to tip her off or scare her off. I wanted this to be a girl to girl talk, not a super to super talk.

I landed on the outskirts of Moon City and walked the rest of the way. Truthfully, it reminded me a lot of Star

Light City. Maybe the houses were painted in slightly darker colors than the houses in Star Light City, but apart from that, it screamed average middle-sized town.

With MAC's GPS, I found 1111 Side Street, a small dead-end street just off Main Street. There were only three houses on the street: 1111, 1110, and 0111. I thought the numbers were a bit strange.

1111 Side Street was a single story, dark green house. It looked very modern with big tinted windows and solar panels on the roof. In fact, it looked a lot like the other houses on the street. The front yard had two big oak trees in it. I don't know much about trees, but I did know that these particular trees had to be older than the house. I walked along a neatly trimmed pavement and up the steps onto the front patio that led to a dark wooden door. I pressed the doorbell. I heard a beep.

"Coming," a young girl's voice called from behind the door. I noticed a camera on the ceiling next to the door. The camera turned to me.

The door popped open. The young girl smiled at me. "Hi!" she said. "We don't get a lot of visitors down this street. Kind of funny. So, I am guessing you are Super Teen, and you want to talk."

I laughed nervously and took a step backward. "ME?" I said pointing to myself, my eyes popping open. "SUPER TEEN? I'm so honored that you would think that." I shook my head and rolled my eyes. "Nope, I'm just simple Lia Smith, from Starlight City. I'm here doing a book report on our neighbor city."

The girl looked at me. "Ah, sure… Lying isn't nice. Did you come to join BAD?"

I laughed again. "Ellie, I assure you I'm not lying. And why would I join anything called BAD."

Ellie's eyes popped open. She leaned on the door. "Cause BAD is good. They help people get better. They cure sick and injured people." She paused. "Wait, if you know my name is Ellie, you must be Super Teen. Right?"

"Lucky guess?"

Ellie looked up at me. "You're a great superhero but a terrible liar!"

Okay, time for a bit of truth. "Actually, I'm a teen reporter for the Sun City paper and blog. A couple of our teens are missing. Rumor has it BAD has them."

Ellie shook her head. "No, BAD wouldn't do something like that."

We both heard a cat crying from above. Ellie walked out the door past me. She looked up in one of the oak trees. Sure enough, we spotted a gray Siamese cat up on one of the top branches.

Ellie looked around. She smiled. "I got this." Ellie started growing, and not normal growth, mind you. She grew to the size of the tree. The now giant Ellie put the cat in her palm and lowered her palm to the ground. The cat hopped off her palm and stretched. Ellie shrank back to normal size.

"So much for being Shrink Girl," I said.

She laughed. "Well even when I grow, I have to shrink again, I can only stay big for a little bit. It really tires me out."

The cat looked at me. The cat opened its mouth. A net flew out of the mouth. The net fell on top of me. Electricity shot through the net burning the ground beneath my feet. I ripped the net off me and tore it into pieces.

"So much for you NOT being Super Teen!" Ellie demanded.

"So much for BAD being good," I replied.

She looked at me. She looked at the cat. "I'm sure it was just trying to protect me. Down kitty!"

The cat stood up, closed one eye and arched its back.

It showed me its claws.

"Not impressed," I told the cat.

The cat crinkled its neck. Its body started to expand. The cat grew to the size of a really large lion.

"Still not impressed!" I said.

The big cat dropped back onto its back paws. You didn't need to be a cat expert to know what its next move would be. The cat pounced towards me, three-inch claws out and glistening in the sunlight. I caught it by the paws before they could hit me.

"Bad kitty!" I said, pinning its claws up in the air and keeping the big cat on two legs. "Give up now!" I said. "I really don't want to hurt you!"

I saw the cat inhale. I did the same thing. It breathed a green smog at me. I held my breath. The smog passed over me. My eyes actually burnt a little. Ellie sighed and fell to the ground. I flung the cat up in the air away from me. The cat thing sprouted wings and hovered above me. It made a hissing sound. It showed me its claws.

I blasted one of its paws with my heat vision. The cat screamed, then flew off.

I lowered myself down to Ellie. I gave her a little shake. I used super breath to blow away the green yuck that still surrounded us. I waved my hand over Ellie. Her eyes popped open.

"They told me you'd come and that they just wanted to talk to you. Ah, okay, maybe BAD isn't so good after all," she said. "I will help you find your friends."

Dear Diary: I think it's safe to say BAD is pretty rotten. They took a nice normal cat and turned it into something that wasn't normal at all. They even tricked Ellie into thinking they were good. At least now I had Ellie on my side. Yeah, I know this could be a trap. Ellie may be pretending to be on my side to get my guard down, but I don't think so. My gut says no, and my brain says listen to my gut.

Oh, I'm also pretty darn pleased with myself that I did learn from my loss to Tanya. As soon as I figured the cat thing might use a breath weapon on me, I prepared. Yes, I may need to breathe like everybody else, but I can hold my breath for a long time. In this case, certainly long enough to get rid of the green toxic gas that spurted out of that cat's mouth. Life lessons can actually be rewarding.

New Friend

"What's your plan?" Ellie asked me.

I looked at her. "I need to get into BAD'S research lab. You know the address, correct?"

Ellie nodded her head. "It's just outside of town, underground. But I can teleport you in. I can even shrink you, so they don't find you. But you have to promise not to hurt anybody."

"I just want to save my friends and get out of there with them," I said.

Ellie looked at me. "I really haven't seen your friends, but there are levels in the lab I'm not allowed in."

"Then that's where I have to go."

"Little cousin, what the heck are you doing?" we heard from behind us.

Turning, I saw Glare Girl standing there with her hands on her hips.

"Oh hi, Martha, I mean Glare Girl," Ellie said. "Why are you here?"

Glare Girl moved towards us. "Does your mom know you're hanging out with people like this?"

"Actually, she does," a voice called from beside us.

We turned to see a short woman with curly dark hair standing on the porch. She had a smile on her face. "I've been listening to the conversation intently. I agree with Ellie and Super Teen."

Glare Girl slammed a foot on the ground. "Oh, Aunt Jeanie! You would take their side! BAD has been good to us. They've cured us and made us super."

"Huh?" I asked.

"I had a gluten allergy," Ellie told me. "The people at BAD made it go away. Plus, I get these cool superpowers!"

"I had acne that wouldn't quit; until I met BAD. Now my skin is perfect. And I'm super."

Jeanie walked off the porch. "I did some legal work for BAD, so I know they aren't all bad." She took a deep breath. "Still, if your friends are missing, I understand the need to check them out."

I didn't know this Jeanie woman, but I had a good feeling about her. I thought I could trust her. I knew the trick here would be getting Glare Girl on our side.

"Look, I don't want them to take away my treatment! I DON'T want acne again!"

Ellie looked up at her, eyes open wide. "I mean, I don't want to have a gluten allergy again either, but I don't want people hurt because of me."

Jeanie put her arm around Ellie. "That's my girl!"

Glare Girl shook her head. "Look, I appreciate your problem, I really do. But that's YOUR problem, not mine. I refuse to go against the people who made me, me."

"As long as you don't get in our way," I said.

Glare Girl shook her head. "I'll try, but I can't lie. If they call me in to help. I am there. I'm not biting the hand that feeds me. I want action, but I'm not stupid."

Time to think this through. I didn't need Glare Girl as an enemy, but I also didn't need her coming to fight me, especially when I might be surrounded by security. Plus, I couldn't let my friends down. I couldn't let anybody stand in my way.

"Okay Glare Girl, you're either with me or against me. And as powerful as BAD may be, trust me, you don't want me as your enemy." I made a fist. "You really don't want to go against me."

Glare Girl took a step back. She squeezed both her fists together. "Well then, I do believe all heroes need an arch-rival." She leaned forward and focused her eyes on me. She squinted.

I felt my body heating up. In fact, my hair started to

crackle with energy.

"Martha, stop!" Ellie pleaded.

"Come on girls, we can work this out," Jeanie said slowly. "Let's all take a step back and collect our breath."

Glare Girl took another step backward. "Why should I stop? I'm winning!"

I took a step back too. I took a slow breath. "You should have taken your aunt's advice."

I thought of the polar ice caps and frozen drinks. I exhaled on Glare Girl. My breath encased her in a block of ice.

"Ha, I've put her on ice!" I laughed.

"Ah, I wouldn't bet on that," Ellie said, pointing at Glare Girl.

Sure enough, her ice block turned red and started to shake. The ice crumpled off her. Heat from her eyes slammed into my shoulder, knocking me down. The glare did pack quite a punch. I leaped up to my feet. I flew through the air and landed on top of Glare Girl, driving her to the ground. She tried to focus her eyes. I covered her eyes with my hand. My hand shook with the pain, but I kept my left hand locked over her eyes. With my right hand, I gave Glare Girl a pinch on the neck. The pressure on my hand stopped, Glare Girl went limp.

I turned to Ellie and her mom. "She shouldn't be a problem now. We should be in and out before she wakes up." I smiled. "Now I just need a good way in. You said you could teleport me in?"

"If you're okay with being shrunk," Ellie said.

"I'm cool with that. I trust you."

Jeanie stepped forward. "You still have a problem. Ellie Mae just can't show up at BAD for no reason. They always call her; she doesn't call them."

"What if I go to visit Dad?" Ellie asked.

Jeanie looked at me. "Her dad, my husband Don, works for their R&D department."

83

"So, he'll know about my friends?"

Jeanie shook her head. "No, he's only involved in the legitimate stuff. He would never condone holding people against their will. Believe me, honey, most of what BAD does is for good. Doctor Dangerfield really wants to help people."

"So, she is in charge?" I asked.

"Yes, very much so."

"Then why is she so secretive?" I asked. "If she's helping people?"

"She claims her experiments are in the very early stages. She doesn't want to go public until she is sure the experiments work for the masses. She also says she's afraid people will try to steal her technology and misuse it. That's why the company is mostly underground," Jeanie laughed. "Most people in this city don't even know BAD exists. If they ask me or my husband, we just tell them we work for a think tank. Which is true."

"How do you get me in there then?" I asked.

"In my purse. While Ellie May can't go there on a whim, we can certainly stop in for a family dinner. Like I said, most of what they do, in fact, everything we see them do, is legitimate and legal, but they do make their staff work long hours. Luckily, they encourage family picnics."

Okay, that certainly didn't sound very evil to me. Still, I had to get in there to see what was up.

"Let's make this so!" I said. I pointed at Glare Girl.

"Great!" Ellie Mae smiled. "I love a picnic and seeing my dad." She pointed at Glare Girl. "But what do we do about her? I love my cousin, but she does have a temper. And she's already waking up from that nerve pinch."

Sure enough, Glare Girl was starting to stir. "Both of you hold your breath!" I said. I raced over to Glare Girl. I popped my foot out of my shoe. She started to push herself up off the ground. I wiggled my toes under her nose. She stopped moving upwards. "OMG!" she sighed. Her eyes rolled to the back of her head. She rolled over holding her throat.

"You didn't kill her, did you?" Ellie asked.

"Nah, she'll just sleep for the rest of the day." I quickly popped my foot back into my shoe before I actually did kill her. I picked her up and carried her into the house.

As I plopped her down on the couch, I got a text from Mom.

MOM>Hey, where r u?

LIA>Chatting with a new friend and her mom.

MOM> Oh, I'm going on another date tonight. Hope ur ok with that?

LIA>NP Mom...I want you to be happy.

MOM>I hope u won't have to save us tonight.

LIA>Ah something tells me Glare Girl won't b a problem 2nght.

Dear Diary: First off, it is amazing how my foot odor is still my most potent weapon. I try not to think too much about that. But, man, when I'm nervous, my feet just sweat, and it's certainly not a sweet sweat. Oh well, Jason tells me it's my body's way of defending itself. I like to think he's right, and it's not that I'm gross.

My fate, and perhaps the fate of Thomas and cute little Felipe, is now in the hands of two people I've just met. I have to hope this isn't a trap. Actually, I know it isn't. I may have just met Ellie Mae Opal and her mom, but I can sense they're good people. I trust my senses. Of course, even with them on my side, I'll still be going into BAD against long odds. Luckily, I'm pretty sure this is nothing Super Teen can't handle. Now, as for my mom dating a reporter who is trying to discover the identity of Super Teen, and my dad dating his android assistant, that's something Lia Strong is going to have to learn to handle. I'm not a kid anymore. Heck, I'm most likely the strongest person in the world. My parents deserve to be happy even if their choices are weird.

Can They Be Trusted?

As Jeanie packed a nice picnic dinner, I made plans with Ellie.

"I'll shrink you, so you fit into our picnic basket," Ellie explained to me.

"They don't check the baskets on the way in?" I asked.

"No," Jeanie answered from the kitchen. "Like I said, BAD is really trusting. As long as you don't wander into the restricted areas."

"You don't find all of that suspicious?" I frowned.

"A lot of companies have restricted areas. BAD says it's because of chemical use and radiation. Until now, I've had no reason to doubt them. Like I said, they have always been good to my family."

I had to think again about whether I was doing the right thing. I was pretty much just putting my fate into the hands of two strangers. Sure, they seemed like very nice people, but they also seemed to really trust BAD. That couldn't be good.

Jeanie walked into the living room carrying the picnic basket. "You look concerned," she said to me.

"BAD has been good to you," I said.

"They have," Jeanie said. "And so now you're worried that we might be bringing you into a trap."

"I'd never do that!" Ellie said.

I put my hand on her shoulder. "I know, Ellie."

"But she can't be totally sure she trusts me," Jeanie said. "After all, I am a lawyer for BAD."

"I want to trust you," I said, looking Jeanie in the eyes.

"Look Super Teen, trust me or not, but I'm your best chance to get into BAD. Sure, Ellie Mae could teleport you in, but security would notice you fairly quickly. Sure, you might be able to take them on, but if your friends are there, they could move them elsewhere pretty quickly. You may not trust me, but I'm still your best chance," Jeanie's eyes were locked on mine.

"She has a valid point," MAC said from my wrist. "Besides, I have been doing a voice analysis of her and she appears to be telling the truth. Either she is being truthful, or she is a fantastic liar!"

Jeanie's eyes jumped open. She pointed at my wrist. "Wow, talk about smartwatches."

I glared at MAC. "Yep, he's smart but a bit annoying at times."

"I just speak the truth!" MAC said.

Jeanie put her hand on my shoulder and looked at me again. "Trust me Super Teen, if BAD is holding people against their will, I will do everything I can to help you free them!"

"They did do a lot to help your daughter and niece," I said.

Jeanie grinned. "Yes, they did, and I am so grateful. But not so grateful that I would let them hurt other innocent people. I would never allow that. Never!"

"Okay," I said with a weak smile.

"You ready to get shrunk?" Ellie Mae Opal asked me. I nodded.

Ellie Mae pointed at me. She squeezed her fingers together. I felt myself shrinking to miniature size.

"Okay, I don't think I'll ever get used to this," I said.

Jeanie leaned over and picked me up. She placed me gently in the basket. "There's some fried chicken for you in there!" she told me.

"Mom, should we drive or teleport there?" Ellie asked.

"Driving is so slow and normal," Jeanie laughed. "Besides, you know the location well!"

A brief moment later, far inside the wonderful smelling picnic basket, I heard Jeanie talking to whom I assume were BAD security people.

"Yes, we're here to have a nice picnic dinner with my husband, Don Opal."

"Have a wonderful evening," I heard the guard say.

I felt myself moving for the first time since I'd been put into the picnic basket. Man, my life was weird. We walked for a bit. I heard an electronic beeping. I assumed it was a code to a door or something. I believe I heard a door slide open.

A man's voice said, "What a pleasant surprise!"

I heard a kiss. Ah, how sweet! The lid to the basket popped open. Jeanie looked in. "You can get out now," she told me.

I leaped out and found myself staring at the surprised face of Ellie's dad.

"Super Teen," Don said. "What's going on here? Is this another training mission like the one in Starlight City? I didn't agree with that... but Doctor Dangerfield insisted no one would get hurt and that it would also be a good experience for Super Teen. Having an arch-rival will inspire her."

"It did kind of inspire me to be better," I admitted.

Ellie pointed at me. I felt myself stretching back to normal size.

"Daddy, she's here to find her friends," Ellie told him. "She says BAD was bad and that they took her friends away."

Don shook his head. "No, BAD wouldn't do that. All the people they recruit are asked to take part in our research. Nobody is forced."

"I'm sure you believe that, but I need to search the place myself, especially the restricted areas!" I said.

The door to the lab opened. In walked Doctor Dangerfield with a couple of security people behind her. The security personnel wore blue body armor.

"Super Teen, if you wanted to visit my lab, all you had to do was ask." Doctor Dangerfield said. She turned to Jeanie. "We scan all packages that come into the complex. We noticed your picnic basket had something special inside of it."

"You can't do that!" Jeanie protested.

"Actually, this is private secure property. We can do it and we certainly do," Doctor Dangerfield said to Jeanie. Doctor Dangerfield turned her attention to me. "Super Teen, my staff and I will gladly give you a tour of our facility. All you have to do is ask."

"'I want to see the restricted area!" I insisted.

Doctor Dangerfield smiled. "I assure you we have no restricted areas here."

"I've seen them," Ellie protested.

Doctor Dangerfield put a hand to her ear, listening to

a headpiece. "My aides assure me those were just for a test simulation they were running. There are no restricted areas here."

Ellie touched me on the shoulder. "Well, one way to make sure…"

A shimmering sphere appeared in front of me. The shimmer cleared to reveal a long black hallway. Ellie grabbed my hand and said, "Come."

We passed into the sphere. We came out in the long black hallway. Red lights lining the hallway started blinking. A robot voice said, "You have entered a restricted area. Please wait to be detained and escorted out."

Four silver hover drones dropped from the ceiling, they looked like electronic beetles. Red dots appeared on both Ellie's shoulders and mine as well. The two front drones fired beams of energy at us from their eyes. A beam hit Ellie, she fell to the ground. A beam hit me. It bounced off me.

"My turn!" I told the four hovering drones.

I leaned forward and focused my heat vision on the drones. They all shattered into pieces. I bent down and picked up Ellie.

"I'm okay," she told me. "She pointed down the hallway. Leave me, they won't hurt me. Check the door at the end of the hall."

I shot down the hallway at super speed. A couple of laser turrets appeared from the walls. They fired at me, but I easily dodged their shots. I noticed a patch of yellow ick on the floor, right before the door. I leaped over it and smashed through the door. I rolled into a huge room with a dome ceiling and just three beds in it. One of the beds held Felipe, another held Tomas, the third held an older woman who I figured had to be Felipe's mom. The three of them had weird rings with diodes on their heads. The diodes were connected to some sort of computer and a big glowing tube. The tube seemed to be filling with golden energy. The three of them

90

laid there unconsciously. I rushed over. I looked at the computer and the tube. Oh my, this went way beyond my eighth-grade science level.

I wanted to just pull off the diodes, but I was afraid that would do more harm. I heard footsteps behind me. Doctor Dangerfield was there along with her security team. The big surprise was Doctor Dangerfield looked as shocked as I did. "What in the name of Newton is this?" she asked.

I took a step forward while pointing at my friends. "You call this volunteering?"

Doctor Dangerfield put her hand on her chest. "Super Teen, you have to believe me... I had no idea what was going on here."

I shook my head. "I find that very hard to believe," I said.

"You can believe her," a voice very much like Doctor Dangerfield's said from behind her.

Another Doctor Dangerfield walked into the room. She was followed by two other Doctor Dangerfields. I'm not sure who looked more shocked, me, the security people or the original Doc Dangerfield.

"C1, are you behind this!" Doctor Dangerfield said, pointing at my friends.

The copy of Doctor Dangerfield grinned. I did not like that grin. "I'm C2," she said.

Doctor Dangerfield shook her head. "You all look alike to me!"

"Doctor Dangerfield, what's going here?" I asked.

Doctor Dangerfield turned to me. "I'm a busy, busy woman. I have a lot to do and quite frankly, I love my research but hate the day-to-day details that go into running a company, so I cloned myself," she said calmly.

"Oh, of course, you did, that sounds SO logical," I said.

"Well, they aren't straight clones of me, they each have bio augment devices in them to help them do even more."

"Oh, that makes it so much better…" I groaned.

Doctor Dangerfield shook her head. "You would not believe the pressure I'm under doing all this. Trying to make the world a better place is hard! With a surprisingly large amount of paperwork involved!"

One of the clones tapped each of the guards on their shoulders. The guards fell to the ground. "That's okay, Doctor," the clone said, "we're now relieving you of all the pressure."

Dear Diary: I'm sure that somehow, some way, there may someday be a use for clones. But man, for a smart woman, Doctor Dangerfield sure did a dumb thing cloning herself. Sure, at times I guess I think it might be cool to have two of me, one to do the homework and regular girl stuff, the other to fight crime or maybe see Brandon. But then I realize it wouldn't be wise to split myself like that. The homework, the boys, the saving the world, the whole package is what makes me, me. There are no shortcuts to a complete life, even when you are super. Looks like Doctor D had to learn this the hard way.

Hard Knocks

Doctor Dangerfield held up her arms. "Wait, you three were only supposed to do the boring stuff I didn't want to do!"

The lead clone laughed. "Sorry, Doc, we've decided to take over. Not just this lab, but eventually everything. We can use these naturally super beings here to supercharge our biodevices, making them even stronger. Soon, everybody in the world will want one of our implants!"

"That sounds so wrong…" I said.

The lead clone cackled. "How is it wrong to make everybody better? They will all be faster, stronger, immune to most diseases…"

"I do not laugh like that!" Doctor Dangerfield insisted.

"Doc stick with the program," I said. I looked at the lead clone. "Okay, what's the catch?"

"Why do you think there's a catch?" the lead clone snickered.

"I do not talk like that!" Doctor Dangerfield insisted. She turned to me. "They want to be able to control the biodevice users."

"Oh, that IS so, so wrong," I said.

"And not anything I wanted," Doc Dangerfield sighed.

The lead clone chuckled. "Ha, you non-bio-enhanced non-clones think so small!"

The second clone stepped forward. "You wanted to make the world a better place and that's what we will be doing. Everybody will be better and under control."

Doc Dangerfield shook her head. "That's not what I

wanted…"

The third clone moved towards her. "Sorry, boring original version of us, you have no say in this matter."

"I created you all!" Doc Dangerfield shouted.

"Yes. But now we have surpassed you. Actually, you should be proud," all three clones said at once. "But since you seem to disagree with our planned course of action, we will put you on ice…" the first clone said. She pointed her hand at Doctor Dangerfield. A thick beam of blue frost hit Doctor Dangerfield. She instantly froze in place, covered in ice.

The clone aimed her hand at me. "Now for you!"

I saw the frozen blue beam coming at me. I jumped up over the beam, diving at the freezing clone. The clone reacted far faster than a normal person, she fired at me again. This time the beam of frost hit me face first. I felt a chill ripple down my entire body, coating me in ice. I spun and spun around like a mini tornado. The ice went flying off me. I crashed down on top of the clone, driving her to ground.

"It will take more than ice to stop me!" I shouted.

The clone smiled up at me. "You certainly are impressive."

"Thank you," I said.

"But you do know we are not alone. Right?"

"I know there are three of you, but I can handle three super clones!" I said bravely.

The clone pointed behind her. "But you might want to look over there."

Looking up, I saw the other two clones smiling. Behind them, I saw about a hundred floating drones that looked like winged metallic crabs, complete with metal claws that glistened to show how razor sharp they were. Each of the drone crabs also had mini-missiles on their backs.

"Those claws can also generate energy beams," the

clone told me.

Before I could react, the drones blasted me with a barrage of missiles and energy beams. The attacks sent me flying backward, slamming into the wall across the room. I slinked down the wall to the floor. My uniform smoked from the firepower they had hit me with.

I got up.

"Not bad," I told the clones and the drones.

The lead clone jumped back to her feet. "Look Super Teen, you are an amazing piece of genetic work. We don't want to hurt you. But you are way outnumbered. Just join our team."

I leaned forward and let the crab drones have it with a full wide blast of heat vision. It felt good to let my powers rip again. It felt even better watching the drones crumble into piles of metallic dust.

"So much for being way outnumbered," I said.

The lead clone held up a finger. "Wait for it."

Each pile of dust started to shimmer. The dust specs began clotting together and growing like metallic blobs of silly putty. Claws and legs sprung out of each blob. The blobs continued their morphing back into metallic drones.

"The drones are made of self-replicating nanobots," the lead clone said. "You can melt them down or freeze them. They will rebuild. They also don't get tired. See, you are outnumbered!"

"She may be outnumbered but she has powerful friends," I heard a familiar voice say.

There, standing behind the clones were Tanya, Jessie, Lori, Marie and Ellie Mae Opal. "I thought you could use your friends," Ellie Mae said.

The lead clone turned towards my team. She thrust a finger at them. "Get them, drones!"

The flying drone crabs turned towards my friends. They started humming with anticipation.

"Take them…

Everything froze in place.

Tanya stood there with her arms outstretched. "Take these things out fast, ladies. I'm not sure how long I can keep that area slowed in time before things start to get dangerous!"

Marie darted forward past Tanya. She concentrated on the mass of killer crab drones. Her chest rose as she took an extra deep breath. She exhaled, aiming her head left and right. As Marie's breath hit each drone, it reduced from shiny metal to dull yellow cheese.

The cheese crab drones plopped to the ground with a squishy splat.

"I'm way hungry," Marie said.

The three clones looked at each other, hands clenched into fists. "Can the nanobots adapt from this?" one of the clones asked.

"Maybe…" the other two said. "Depends on how deeply that girl's power changed them."

Jess walked up towards the clones. "Sorry, they won't get a chance." She looked at me. "Can I vanish these?"

I grinned. "Yes please."

Jess turned to a corner of the room and clasped her hands together. She slowly separated her hands. A rift appeared across the room seeming to cut into reality itself. The rift slowly rolled open, revealing a deep black emptiness. Jess pointed at the cheese drones and then waved towards the rift. The drones floated off the ground and flew into the dark emptiness. Jess clapped her hands closed. The rift slammed shut as if it wasn't ever there.

The three clones exchanged worried glances. "What do we do now?" one of them asked. "We were prepared for Super Teen, but not all of these Super Teens."

Lori sprang forward on her bionic legs, landing between the three clones.

"What you do now is you all go to sleep!" Lori said. She walloped the lead clone in the jaw. The bionic punch sent the clone staggering backward, her head popping back.

The clone spat out a tooth. "Not bad, but it will take more than that to stop us. You and your friends have impressive power, but I'm guessing the time controller, the witch, and the molecular controller are all worn out from using their powers! And they are no match now for the three of us super clones!"

"Ha!" Lori said with a stomp of her foot. "My friends are just warming up!"

"Actually, I'm beat," Marie said. "Turning everything to cheese is hard!"

"I might be able to slow time a bit, but that trick also drained a lot of me," Tanya admitted.

"I still have power to spare!" Jessie said, she raised her arms over her head. Her hands crackled with yellow energy. The energy sizzled then fizzled out with a puff of smoke. Jessie dropped her arms to her sides. "Okay, maybe not..." she said slowly. She sniffed herself and curled her nose. "But I did manage to burn out my deodorant."

"See, I told you!" the lead clone said, pointing to her head. "We are really smart."

Lori took a fighting stance. "I will take you all out myself then."

The three clones snickered. "You don't stand a chance!"

Doc Dangerfield jumped between the clones and Lori. She held her arms up. "Wait, I made you so you could help make the world better!"

The lead clone shrugged. "We are; it is just that our idea of "better" differs from yours."

Doc Dangerfield dropped down into a fighting stance. "Then you must fight me too!"

The clone sighed. "Original us, you are in great shape for a non-enhanced being, but no match for us!"

"Ha, but you're my clone, I programmed you so you can't hurt me!" the good doctor smiled.

The clone nodded. "True," she pointed at the other two clones. "But they aren't your clones, they are my clones. They can hurt you."

The two others nodded readily in agreement.

"Oops, loophole," Doctor D said.

I stomped my foot on the floor, sending a shockwave rippling through the surface that knocked over everybody else in the room.

"You probably shouldn't forget me. You know...Super Teen."

The three clones jumped back to their feet. "Yes, our niece Wendi is right. She has such an ego."

"She's my niece, not yours!" Doc Dangerfield said.

I rolled my eyes. "Please, she is so wro- "

The three clones leaped across the room at me. "See, my fellow clones? I knew talking about our niece would distract her!"

They landed on top of me, pushing me to the ground. They were right. They did make me mad talking about Wendi like that. I filled with anger. And when I got angry, I tended to burn through my deodorant. I grabbed two of the clones and stuck their noses right under my arms. The two struggled for a bit. They fought to break my grip, my scent was too strong. Heck, I could smell it myself. I actually thought it had the aroma of a pleasant cheese. I guess the clones didn't agree. The two clones, with their noses locked in my armpit, sighed then went limp. The third clone, the leader, leaped up off me.

"You won't put me down that easily, Super Teen!" she said.

Lori tapped the clone on her shoulder, and the clone turned. Lori hit her with a jab to her jaw. The clone stumbled towards me. I rolled the other two clones off me and jumped to my feet. I caught the stumbling clone. I tapped her on the forehead. She fell over stiff. I blew on my finger.

Doc Dangerfield ran up to me. "Super Teen, I am so

sorry. I never meant for any of this to happen! I only wanted clones to help with the workload, not to take over the world."

I pointed to Felipe, his mom, and Tomas laying on the strange beds. "Yeah, well, we all make mistakes. If my friends are okay, I guess there's no real harm done."

"Right, I'll wake them up now!"

I watched as Doctor D went over and removed Felipe, his mom and Tomas from the devices they had attached to them. Felipe hugged me. Tomas hugged Jess. Doctor D promised us that with the help of her security people, she would keep the clones on ice so they couldn't cause any more trouble. All was good with the world. We had stopped three crazy clones from taking over. It felt good to be me. Once I saw Felipe, Tomas, and Felipe's mom were all okay, I thanked my team and we all headed home.

When I got home I got a text from Jason.

JASON> I heard u did great.

LIA>Thanks.

JASON>Wish I could have been there but ur dad said it would be too dangerous for me.

LIA>Sorry bud. I missed u but I do need to be able to fight super bad guys without u. Just so I learn.

JASON>Well I did my share by helping for tmw.

LIA>Tmw?

JASON>Ur speech in front of the entire school.

LIA>NO!!!!!!! I so forgot.

JASON>Yeah u were busy saving the world and all.

LIA>OMG!!! I just took a shower and I'm sweating again! It might knock out the block!

JASON>Don't worry u'll be great. U just need to let the other kids know ur a nice normal person who has their best interests at heart.

LIA>Really? Me normal?

JASON>Lia, we've been through this, mentally ur as

normal as they come. Though, I think u better go take another shower. I just noticed all the birds in the trees between our houses have passed out!

Dear Diary: I try not think too hard about the fact that my scent can overpower super-powered clones. Or, for that matter, knock out all the birds in the area. I consider it just another weapon I can use to stop crime. It's amazing that despite all my powers, the thing in this world that still bothers me the most is Wendi Long. Oh well, I guess it's nice to be super, but still have to deal with regular problems. If I am going to win this election, it will be because I am mostly normal.

Speech Morning

The next morning, I found Mom and Dad both there to greet me at the breakfast table. Now, I'd always had breakfast with Mom, it was our thing, but Dad being there was new.

"What's the matter? Did Grandma Betsy get hurt or something?" I asked.

Mom shook her head and motioned for me to sit at the table. "No all is fine."

I sat down in front of a breakfast of pancakes with blueberries, fried potatoes, fresh pineapple and raspberries, and bacon, lots of bacon. (One of the cool things about being super, is that I do burn a lot of calories throughout the day.)

"Wait, why are all my favorite foods here?" I asked.

"You had a big day yesterday," Dad said. "Taking out the clones and the drones."

"I had help," I said. "My team kicked it up."

"True," Dad acknowledged. "But you're still the leader and the face of the team. You're the only one who has gone public with their powers."

"I don't mind," I said, nibbling on nice crispy bacon. "I was born to be a hero. All my women ancestors have been super. I mean, Lori and Marie were made super by experiments that they didn't even really agree to. Tanya and her little sister are super because of a nuclear accident. Cute little Ella Mae Opal was altered to be super. And Jessie, well she's just different."

"That's what's really super about you," Dad smiled. "How you live up to being super."

"Plus, we want to talk to you about love lives," Mom

said slowly.

"Oh, so gross mom. I'm eating here!"

"I mean, it can't be that easy for you, me dating a reporter who wants to learn your secret identity, and your dad dating a woman that he literally made."

"Hey, what's wrong with that?" Dad asked turning to Mom.

"So many things," Mom sighed.

"Look, guys, any kid thinks the idea of their parents going on dates is weird, no matter who they are dating. It's just how life goes. But really, all I care about is you guys being happy!" I told them.

"Thanks," Mom said, putting her hand on my arm. "You're a great kid!"

"I appreciate it too, and so does Hana," Dad said. "And to repeat, I don't see anything strange about me dating an android who is human in almost every way."

"Actually Dad, the only really strange thing is that she seems to get human nature better than you do," I snickered. It was kind of a joke, but also not a joke.

Dad looked at me. He slumped back in his chair. "Yeah, I get that, but I'm trying."

I put my hand on dad's arm. "Thanks, Dad, I appreciate the effort."

"Plus," Mom said, even slower, "you have a big event at school today."

I turned away. "Oh, do I? I have hardly thought of it."

Suddenly I had a hiccup. And when I say a hiccup, I really meant the up part. The hiccup forced me up into the air, I banged into the ceiling, putting a huge dent in it. I dropped to the ground, smashing the wooden chair I'd been sitting on into pieces.

"What the heck—" Another hiccup sent me flying up and down again, putting another hole in the ceiling and grinding the wooden chair to dust.

"Honey take a deep breath," Mom said.

"Those are nervous hiccups, you had them when you were younger," Dad said.

Mom turned to Dad. "I'm surprised you remember?"

"Look, I know I wasn't the world's greatest dad, but I remember things."

"Guys," I quivered. "Help me before I destroy the kitchen."

Mom put her hand on my back. "Like I said honey, breathe in."

I took a deep breath in.

"Now let it out!"

I exhaled, sending Dad flying across the kitchen. He crashed into the wall. He fell to the floor. He laid there out cold.

"Oops," I said.

Mom started to laugh harder than I had ever seen her laugh before. She actually doubled over with laughter. "Oh honey, I can't believe you did that, but I am so glad you did."

Mom paused for a second and wiped a tear out of her eye. "I obviously still have issues with your dad. I mean, come on, the man is dating an android."

"I know it's weird Mom, but he's happy. Plus, she keeps him grounded."

Mom bent down and hugged me. "That's why I love you. Your spirit is as strong as any of your powers."

I noticed the hiccups were gone. "I'm hiccup-free!" I said.

Mom nodded. "Yeah, they're a nervous reaction, and you're not nervous any longer." Mom looked me in the eyes. "Trust me, honey, you're going to be fine."

Dear Diary: Wow! Just when I thought I'd run out of embarrassing super-powers, I discovered super destructive hiccups. Man, those aren't fun. I just need to stay relaxed, and I will be fine. Who would have thought that my dad dating an android would be one of the more normal events of my life?

Speech Time

The day flew by. Pretty much the next thing I knew, I was sitting up on stage in the school auditorium. Jason, as my campaign manager, sat beside me. School Vice Principal MACadoo stood at a podium in the middle of the stage and he was going on and on about the importance of elections in our society. I didn't mind because the more he talked, the more time I had to wait.

Across from me sat Wendi and her campaign manager Patti. Wendi looked so smug wearing a red dress with a red jacket on top of it. She had a flag pin on her collar. I swore her dress had to be extra short. That Wendi would do anything to get a vote. I couldn't blame her; she did have really good legs! Wendi sat there looking at VP MACadoo and smiling.

That's when it hit me again. I knew I was about to experience another super hiccup attack. I stood up.

"Where are you going?" Jason asked me.

"I've got a personal problem…" I said hurriedly. I started off the stage, hoping nobody would notice.

"Ms. Strong, where are you going?" VP MACadoo asked.

"Sorry sir, nature calls!" I said.

The entire school student body laughed.

I streaked off the stage. Once I got out of the view, I ran at super speed into the girls' bathroom. If I was going to have a super hiccup attack, I'd do it out of sight. Luckily, the entire school was at the speeches. Well, not so lucky, since they all now were laughing at me.

I raced into the bathroom so fast I almost ran into Janitor Jan who was wiping some writing off of one of the stalls. Good thing Jan saw me coming, so she levitated out of the way. Jan dropped back to the floor.

"Lia, what are doing in here? You should be giving a speech now."

"Sorry, Jan, I had a nervous attack. I had to get out of there before I did something bad."

"What?" Jan said.

"HICCUP!" I shot up to the ceiling, cracking it. I fell back down on the floor, denting the floor.

"That…" I said.

Jan shook her head. "Girl, I just washed this floor." Jan put her hands on my shoulders. "Now you have to calm down. Don't make me turn you into a gel pad for my shoes."

"Say what?" I said.

Jan grinned. "When somebody does something that messes up my school, I teach them a lesson. I turn them into a gel pad and stick them in my shoes. Right now, Cindy Love is in my right shoe due to that heart she drew on the wall. That big bully, Tony Wall, is in my left shoe due to dropping papers all over the school. The kid doesn't seem to care." Jan reached down and pulled off her right shoe. There inside was a flattened little blond girl, Cindy Love.

"Jan please put your shoe back on," I asked.

Jan laughed. "Yeah, they can pack quite the kick. You're lucky you're super or you probably would have been out for the count."

"How long do you keep people in your shoes?"

"Just a couple of hours to teach them a lesson. They don't remember anything once I turn them back. They just know not to litter or clutter the school again. It's really a human service," Jan insisted.

"Ah, okay," I said. I noticed my hiccups had stopped. "Hey, I'm okay now!"

Jan smiled. "Yeah, you've calmed down."

"Do you have some magic that can keep me calm?" I asked her.

"I do. It's the best magic of all." Jan put her hand on

my shoulder. She looked me in the eyes. "Just trust yourself. You're a good kid. You're smart, and you try to do the right thing. Just tell your classmates that and you'll be fine."

"Really?" I said.

Jan shrugged, "I sure hope so. If not, just hit them all with a super fart and none of them will remember a thing when they come to," Jan laughed, leading me to the door. "Now get back and give them a great speech. Knock em dead! Just figuratively of course!"

I skulked back into the auditorium as Wendi gave her speech. She must have been talking for a few minutes already but that didn't stop her from rambling on. She talked about her accomplishments, being a class homecoming queen, being a straight-A student, being the star of the LAX team. How she could help lead our school into even better times. She would work on longer lunch breaks, improving the boys' LAX teams, and getting a student lounge. She concluded that she was the only person to lead our class. She did mention that I was so afraid to speak I was probably in the bathroom crying.

The class laughed. I fought back the urge to remove my shoes and clobber them all with super foot odor.

VP MACadoo took the podium and introduced me.

I stood up. I walked slowly to the podium. "Thank you VP MACadoo," I said. I saw Jason give me a thumbs up. I turned to my classmates.

"My fellow classmates. What can I say? I'm not perfect like Wendi. I don't have perfect hair or the perfect complexion. I have bad hair days. I get zits. I get nervous when I'm about to speak in front of a bunch of people. So, if you want somebody perfect, you really should vote for Wendi. But, if you want somebody who can relate to you and will be there for you, please vote for me. I may not be the best, but I do promise I will have all of your best interests at heart. Thank you."

I walked off of the podium, and the class started to

clap. I smiled.

VP MACadoo took the podium. "Well, students, you've heard the candidates, and you may all vote before leaving the auditorium. Votes need to be handed to Miss Mayfield on your way out. She will be doing the counting."

I glanced towards the school administrator, Miss Mayfield, and realized that my fate was in her hands.

As I sat down, the reality of the situation hit me. I leaned into Jason. "Wait, the vote is today?"

He smiled. "Yes, and you did great."

Dear Diary: Fighting a group of super clones and drones was nearly as nerve-racking as having to speak in front of my class. I did my best. I just had to hope the class related to me.

Speech Wrapped

At the end of the day, both Jason and I were getting ready to leave school.

"Lia wait!" I heard a voice call.

I saw Steve running towards me. "Lia! You won!" he said.

"Won what?" I asked.

"Class president!" Steve said. "I'm in charge of tabulating the vote since I'm so good with numbers. You won by over 20 votes. It won't be announced until the morning, but I wanted to tell you."
"Gee thanks, Steve, I really appreciate it."

Jason and I headed out of the school with Steve walking with us. "Ah, Steve, don't you live on the other side of town?" I asked.

"Yes, I do. But I like the extra walk, it's good for me. I'm in great shape you know. I run cross-country. Plus, since I'm class treasurer and class secretary we'll be working together this year."

"That's nice," I said.

"So, I thought it would be fun if I got to know you better."

We walked on for a while. With Steve asking me everything from my favorite color to my favorite food, to my favorite author, to my favorite show. He asked me a lot of stuff.

Jason answered most of the questions for me. I believe Jason wanted to prove that he knew me better than anybody. I'm not totally sure, but I may have detected a bit of jealousy on Jason's part. He didn't appreciate another boy butting in on his time.

Steve stopped walking with us. His eyes glazed over. "I just remembered," he said slowly. "I have to go home now and wash my underwear. After all, I've worn this underwear all week now."

Steve turned and ran off.

"Did you make him say that?" Jason asked.

"Ah, no," I said. "Though it was tempting…."

"I did!" A voice said from above.

Looking up, I saw a cute boy with curly red hair and

big green eyes floating in a tree above us. He slowly lowered himself to the ground. He held out his hand. "Lia Strong, I am Zeekee Zaxxx from the planet ZZZ-333, and I need your help!"

Just when I thought my life couldn't get any more interesting, it did!

The end, for now….

***

Many thanks to our readers and editors: Tayah, Kristin, and Ruby!

Thank you for reading our Super Girl series!
Find out what happens next in…

Super Girl Book 5

OUT NOW!

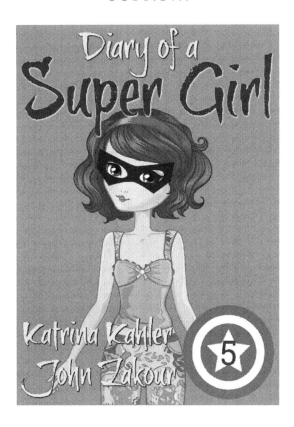

Here are some of our most popular books…

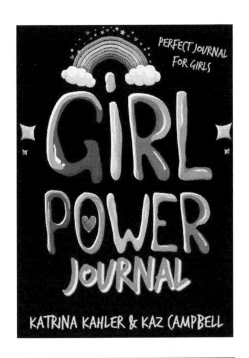

About the Authors

John Zakour is a humor / SF/ fantasy writer with a Master's degree in Human Behavior. He has written thousands of gags for syndicated comics, comedians and TV shows (including Simpsons and Rugrats and, Joan River's old TV show.) John has written seven humorous SF novels for Daw books (the first The Plutonium Blonde was named the funniest SF book of 2001 by The Chronicle of Science Fiction). John has also written three YA books, four humorous self-help books and three books on HTML. John has also optioned two TV shows and three movies. His books may be found here: http://www.amazon.com/John-Zakour/e/B000APS2F0

Katrina Kahler is the Best Selling Author of several series of books, including Julia Jones' Diary, Mind Reader, The Secret, Diary of a Horse Mad Girl, Twins, Angel, Slave to a Vampire and numerous Learn to Read Books for young children. Katrina lives in beautiful Noosa on the Australian coastline. You can find all of Katrina's books here: Best Selling Books for Kids

Made in the USA
San Bernardino, CA
11 May 2020